TO THEIR HEART'S DESIRE

SINFULLY DAMNED SERIES

LESLIE BATES

Editor: Taylor Robinson

Proofreader: Taylor Robinson

Interior Designer: Kristen Hamilton

Cover Designer: Ever After Cover Designs

Character Art: Vii Morte

TRIGGER WARNINGS

IMPORTANT NOTE

Sex trafficking is the most common type of trafficking in the U.S.

Child sex trafficking has been reported in all 50 U.S. States.

Human trafficking is a $150 billion industry.

Human trafficking is the second most profitable illegal industry in the U.S.

https://ourrescue.org/education/research-and-trends/human-trafficking-statistics

With every purchase of To Their Hearts Desire, I will be donating 5% of its profits to The Exodus Project quarterly.

You can help lower these statistics by educating yourself on the signs of human trafficking and reporting anything suspicious to local authorities.

"There are two tragedies in life: one is to lose your heart's desire. The other is to gain it."
- George Bernard Shaw

This is for the girls who were told they were too much - too loud, too emotional.
Don't ever stop speaking up for yourselves.

PLAYLIST

You can listen to the full playlist at

https://open.spotify.com/playlist/
7JcYscY1hM5VvE64VUuUen?si=
_2M5JVV6TImFlRluqRF6zg

Keep an eye out for footnotes to pair specific scenes to the songs that inspired them listed in this playlist. I'd recommend playing the songs on repeat/until the end of the chapter or until an ornamental break for a more immersive reading experience.

CHAPTER ONE

EMILIA

THE SPLATTER OF MY BODYGUARD'S BLOOD PAINTED MY FACE AS I watched the bullet tear through his head. The bullet had come so close to hitting its mark that I had felt the ripple of its path of destruction as it glided through the calming air. Another shot rang through the night, and my other bodyguard dropped to the ground, a perfect kill shot through his skull, the echo of glass shattering still ringing in my ear. This was the fifth time this month someone had tried to kill me, but that wasn't at all shocking, not in my line of work as a mafia queen.* What did surprise me was that they had managed to get to me undetected, unnoticed. In those five childish attempts someone had made to kill me, it had been them that ended up buried in an unmarked grave, and it was always by the sleight of my hand.

I didn't feel terror at the threat upon my life; in fact, I felt the adrenaline spike in my heart at the thrill of the hunt. Emilia DeLuca was a household name in the city of Chicago, known for being dangerous and lethal. I was a walking target in this city, and I sure as hell enjoyed being chased.. Men in

---

* Dark Side - Bishop Briggs

three-piece suits whirred past, taking cover and ladies dressed in the finest silk screamed around me.

People referred to me as the *Serpent Queen*, as I had a reputation among elite society for being manipulative and deceptive when it came to those who crossed me. I never hesitated. I struck hard and fast—hence the name I was given. Although I'd like to believe it was because of the serpent tattoo that covered a good portion of my skin. Regardless, my name and status got me noticed by many different groups of people—FBI, powerful men, and now an elite secret society. They called themselves the *Septem Daemonia*—the seven devils. They thrived in the shadows, and tonight was my initiation. My first task was simple - choose a location, pick one of the seven deadly sins to embody and set the scene. Invites would be sent out the day of, with just the address and the instructions. I had chosen envy. It made the most sense, since it was a sin that I evoked the most out of people. I was beautiful, rich, powerful, and feared.

The event I was hosting lay just on the outskirts of Chicago, located on a 1200-acre property that overlooked a majestic lake and endless woods. The Armada House was the perfect location to bring my fantasy to life: a masquerade ball I called *This Side of Heaven*.

The Armada House embodied the perfect blend of luxury and elegance that I was going for, from the ornate grand staircase to the manicured garden and the beautiful pergola that overlooked the reflective pool. And I looked every bit a sinner in my emerald silk gown. The cut of my dress fell low, my breasts spilling out in the middle, covered only by a scrap of material.

There was a giant slit on the side that ran up the length of my thigh, and just hidden a little higher up my leg was my gun. My dress fell dangerously low in the back, revealing my serpent tattoo that traveled the length of my spine, the head of the snake resting just on the side of my neck. With my dark green feathered mask to complete the look, I was the devil incarnate.

The night was still young, and only moments ago my esteemed guests were enjoying themselves quite intimately. Floor-to-ceiling windows surrounded them, the light of the full moon casting a ghostly presence. The room itself channeled decadence with an exuberance of gold and green decor.

A musician played jazz music down the hall, its sweet, rich melody floating down toward the guests and whisking people into a trance. Women walked around, their bodies dripping in gold glitter as it painted them like a second skin. Some of them held trays of champagne, while others danced on a dais for pure entertainment. Food lined the buffet table off to the side, filled to the brim with sweets and foreign delicacies. As I walked through the crowd, shadows danced along the walls, the hanging candelabras only providing so much light. I grabbed another champagne glass from a passing tray and brought it up to my lips. Three women off to my left captured my attention when their not-too-subtle conversation graced my ears. They were drunk, which made them undeniably bold in their words but also loud and irritating.

"There she is," the woman dressed in a full length maroon gown whisper-yelled to her friend in the black cocktail dress.

"I heard she ripped a guy's dick off because he looked at her funny," the third woman dramatically drawled in a Southern accent.

I scoffed, a coy smile forming from behind the flute of champagne wrapped in my hand. *I mean, they weren't half wrong,* I thought. I didn't rip the guy's dick off, no; I went for his heart. And it wasn't due to him looking at me in some type of way. No, I ripped the man's heart out because he disrespected me by laying a hand on me. There was a difference.

All three pairs of eyes went wide when I walked right up to them, inserting myself into their conversation.

"It was actually his heart," I tell them, downing the last of my champagne. "And it was delicious," I finished with a dramatic wink.

They quickly dispersed, their faces scrunched up, pure judgement in their eyes and disgust portrayed on their faces. Women didn't really like me much. Even at thirty-two, I couldn't figure out if it was my charming personality or my beautiful figure that made them envy me to the point of loathing.

But despite what those women thought of me, to be invited to one of my scandalous parties was a privilege; everyone knew they were legendary. People flocked to my parties, even those without an invite begging for a crumb of entertainment, regardless of my notorious reputation. This party would be no different. The location, the decor, the vibes —my party planner had brought my vision to life, and it was an absolute sight to behold. Until now. This assassin had ruined my night and chance of initiation into the *Septem Daemonia*. If I could have the support and backing of the *Septem Daemonia*, it would make my life easier. People speculated who was part of the "popular boys' club", some whispering that powerful political figures, dirty law enforcement, and even celebrities made up this selective group.

The sound of Dante, my second-in-command screaming frantically into an earpiece next to me, jarred me back to the present, as he moved in closer to my back. I didn't have a chance to get my bearings as I was half-dragged to a nearby exit.

I felt a burning sensation light up my skin like a raging inferno as a bullet sliced through my upper arm. I grimaced at the stinging bite of fire it left in its wake, but I had been shot before; I could withstand a graze like this. All he had managed to do was piss me off. Rolling my eyes and with the rush of adrenaline I got at the thought of death, I shoved my under-boss off and looked up through my long eyelashes, peering out into the dark with a deadly look as I stepped closer to death's fingertips, daring the assassin to take another shot.

I almost hoped he would.

I didn't know if that made me brave or crazy—maybe a little bit of both. When I saw the infrared light from the assassin's gun travel up my body in a seductive caress, I smiled and winked, just as it settled directly in the middle of my forehead. I didn't move. Instead, I squared my shoulders and lifted my chin slightly, fearless in the face of death. I brought my pointer and middle finger up and with my fingers shaped like a gun, I took aim into the darkness, just as the sound of a shot reverberated in the night.

Someone tackled me to the ground, a warm body shielding me from the bullet that was gunning for me. Shouts rang out all around me as my team swarmed me and my dark angel dressed in an all-black Tom Ford three-piece suit. I was captivated by the most devastating green eyes, as they sparkled like an emerald, underneath his sheer black mask. The stranger's lips ever-so-slowly lifted in a smile.

"Have a death wish now, do we, *diavolessa*?"

His voice was a lullaby, a deep angelic voice that serenaded my ears, a lilt of an accent creeping its way to the front.

"I don't fear death; it should fear me," I replied, my blood-red lips curling into a sinister smile.

He chuckled quietly to himself and as he lifted his body off of mine, I noticed the rip in his suit and the blood that pooled down his arm. This stranger, with the beautiful and enchanting eyes that swallowed me whole like a dark and mysterious forest, had taken a bullet for me.

"You're injured." I reached up to grab his arm, and the second I made contact, it's like time warped and slowed down, his touch sending a shockwave through my fingertips. He blinked once, then twice, and there was a slight dilation of his pupils before he cleared his throat.

He looked down briefly at the hole in his suit and shrugged.

"Just a flesh wound, amore. I'll survive," he said in a voice soft with indifference.

Dante pulled me from the marble tile and dragged me back into an alcove, away from any windows or doors. I heard faint mumbling in his earpiece as my car pulled up to the front doors.

I held up my hand to Dante, a noise of irritation falling from his lips, but I ignored him.

"And do I have the honor of knowing who my knight in dark armor is?"

The beautiful stranger took my hand in his, and I felt an electric current shoot through my arm again at his touch, as he slowly lowered himself to kiss my hand. That's when I drank in all his details: the tattoos that covered the tops of his hands like gloves, and the ones crawling up his neck. I would bet that underneath that fitted suit, I would find more tattoos than skin, and I had the sudden urge to drag my hands up and down that artwork. I bit my lip, thinking about where my traitorous thoughts had been drawn to as he gave me a look of amusement then, as if he could read my thoughts too.

"Matteo," was all he managed to relay, before Dante shoved me under his arm and rushed me to the armored vehicle that lay waiting for me. When I was safely inside the car, I peered out the tinted windows, hoping to catch a glimpse of Matteo once more, only to prove to myself he wasn't a figment of my imagination, but he had already disappeared like a phantom in the breeze.

CHAPTER TWO

MATTEO

GETTING SHOT TONIGHT HAD NOT BEEN PART OF MY ELABORATE plan, but no one could say I wasn't dedicated to my job. As soon as Emilia DeLuca escaped into the night, I slipped out a side door and ran through the woods where an unregistered van awaited. I pushed my way inside, slamming the door behind me, only to be greeted by an onslaught of curse words.

"I could've killed you, you fucking idiot!" Tobias chastised me from the front. He was dressed in all black, as he put the van in drive and made his way back to the city.

I fingered the hole in my suit and swore. I liked that suit.

"You ruined a very expensive suit!"

"You're the fool that jumped in front of a bullet not meant for you."

I chuckled, pulling my shirt off and began to remove the bullet from my shoulder with tweezers from the emergency kit with a grimace. Once the bullet was out, I cleaned the wound, before dressing it with a bandage. I threw my shirt back on, leaving it unbuttoned, the movement jostling my tender shoulder.

I was used to physical pain. In fact, I craved it. It not only reminded me that I was alive, but deep down, I knew I deserved to feel every stab wound, every bullet that pierced my skin, and every punch thrown at me. It was my punishment and yet my redemption. The distant groans and screams of my men and the bright flames of destruction burned their way through my memory, ingraining themselves into my soul. A nightmare I could never escape from.

Physical pain I could withstand, but the emotional and mental part crippled me. I shut down my thoughts, every feeling of regret and remorse, and willed myself to forget that particular night. The memory faded from my mind like mist from a thunderstorm, but I knew it would crawl its way forward once more. I shook my head, as if trying to shake the past away, and focused back on my friend driving up front.

"It's a good thing you're a shit sniper," I replied, my voice dripping with sarcasm. Tobias Gialelis was the best sniper my gun-for-hire business had in its arsenal, so I knew without a doubt Tobias's shot would've hit his target if I had not intervened. It was never our intention to kill the *Serpent Queen*, but I knew Tobias wouldn't have been able to resist her taunt. He had always been trigger-happy back in our military days. If anyone understood the nightmares that plagued me, it was Tobias. He had lived through that day too, although neither of us would bring it up to each other.

Despite me getting shot tonight, our plan had worked. I was on Emilia's radar, and it would only be a matter of time before she grew impatient as to who I was, and I'd be ready for her.

It wasn't long before Tobias and I pulled into the underground garage at FBI headquarters. I hopped out of the van, swiftly buttoning up the rest of my shirt before entering the building.

"You know Supervisory Special Agent Richards isn't going to be too pleased that we improvised tonight," Tobias admitted, as the elevator took us up to the 12th floor.

I didn't bother to look his way when he spoke up.

"If he wanted this by the books, he shouldn't have hired outside contractors for the job," I stated, a smug look crossing my face.

The elevator came to an abrupt stop, and the doors opened to reveal a bustling office filled with field agents poring over documents, and techs typed viciously across keyboards, never once looking away from their computer screens. It was all mundane to me. No adrenaline rush, no thrill, no danger— I hated the thought of ever being behind a desk.

We made our way to the corner office that housed SSA Richards. From the window I could see that he was on the phone, one hand on his hip, the muscles in his jaw tense. I had a distinct feeling this would be about my theatrical hero move. SSA Richards looked up and spotted me, and I swore his gray eyes darkened to the color of a summer thunderstorm. He narrowed his eyes at the two of us and summoned us into his office with a flick of his hand.

The two of us entered the office, and we each took a seat in the uncomfortable gray leather chairs. I took in SSA Richards as he nodded to whatever the other person was saying on the other line. Judging from the look that plagued his face, it was not a good conversation.

He had short, salt and pepper hair slicked back, and his gunmetal gray eyes were those of someone who had seen too much in their line of work. They seemed haunted—that much I could tell. I always did my research on the clients I worked with, and from what I had gathered, SSA Richards had been

9

handsome back in his younger days, but the job had worked him to the bone, the bags under his eyes as dark as the night sky and weighing heavily on the man's face.

I knew of Richards's reputation even when I was working in the military. He was once a lethal field agent, until a wound confined him to working the desk, but with his status and skill set he had worked his way to the seat he currently occupied now. SSA Richards was a man to be respected, and even at his age, he was just as deadly.

SSA Richards hung up the phone, bowing his head in defeat, and exhaled a deep sigh. His silver eyes took us in and he shook his head, disappointed.

Here it comes, I thought.

Richards came around to the front of his desk and perched himself up against it, his ankles crossing as he folded his arms over his chest.

"Want to explain to me why I just got off the phone with Director Wheeler about how an assassin took a shot at killing Miss Emilia DeLuca? And not only that, but why is your face, Matteo, plastered all over social media and news outlets saving her?"

I went to answer him, but SSA Richards interrupted me before I could get a word out.

"That was a rhetorical question, Ricci, I do not require an answer from you. It seems that you two went off book on this one. This was supposed to be a hit on her bodyguards, a scare tactic to push Emilia to acquire your services, Matteo, not a hit on *her*," he scolded, before fixing his eyes on me. His eyes then drift to the man sitting next to me. "And you, Gialelis— what on Earth were you thinking, taking a headshot at the Donna of the Italian mafia? We need to be strategic; this is a calculated game of chess, boys, not checkers that we are playing. Think next time before you pull the trigger." The end of his rant was directed at Tobias.

I respected SSA Richards, but I didn't envy his position. If things had gone differently for me in my military career, I could've seen myself working for the FBI officially, making my way through the ranks, but fate had other plans for me. But, as it was, I didn't *officially* work for the FBI. Tobias and I were outside contractors that official government agencies hired when they wanted to "bend" the rules they adhered to. A loophole, per se. After my military stint, I formed a militia group that targeted criminals by whatever means necessary. We had over two hundred employees now and my home base was originally down in Texas, but I had intentions of expanding to other regions. This is what the FBI hired me and my team to do. Improvisation was vital in our line of work, and honestly, screw SSA Richards. The FBI had been trying to nail Emilia DeLuca for years on weapons trafficking, money laundering, and political corruption, hoping something would stick, but they had failed thus far. My team was the last resort, so this was my operation, not theirs. And it was about time I reiterated that to the suits who thought they were in charge.

I stood to my full height of 6'2" and buttoned my jacket, preparing to leave. "With all due respect sir, this is my operation. This is what you hired me to do. You hired me for a position that none of your agents can do. My team and I can. We do what no agent has the stomach or mental capacity to do. Improvisation is how we work, and if you or the Bureau can't get behind that fact, then maybe you should consider terminating our contract and your organization can *try* to dismantle DeLuca's crime organization legally."

Tobias looked up at me, eyes slightly wide.. I stood taller, shoulders drawn back. Tobias stood up, following my lead. We started to make our way to the door when SSA Richards groaned from his desk.

"Just try to stay out of the news."

My hand halted on the door handle and I looked over my shoulder and smirked.

"No promises."

CHAPTER THREE

EMILIA

WE MADE IT BACK TO MY ESTATE IN HALF OF THE TIME IT normally would have taken. Dante didn't want to give my would-be assassin a chance to follow us from the Armada House. My heels clicked on the white Italian marble that I had personally flown over from Italy when Dante came barreling in behind me.

"Are you out of your damn mind?"*

I pivoted where I stood, taking him in. He had dirty blonde hair that was slicked back, his hazel eyes narrowing in on me, silently fuming. He was muscular and in shape, with broad shoulders and robust arms. If anyone else on my team had spoken to me like that, I would have cut out their tongue for their insolence, but Dante, well, I had a soft spot for him.

We had grown up together, friends before we both unintentionally fell into this life of violence and loneliness. He was the person I trusted the most with my life, so the induction into the secret society and not being able to loop him in weighed heavily on my mind. I peered down at him, though

---

* Control - Halsey

he was taller than me, even in my stiletto heels. He lowered his eyes in shame.

"I'm sorry, Emmy." His voice was apologetic, the slip of his nickname for me melting my stoic facade and forcing a soft smile to break to the surface for him. His hand came up to rub his chin, and he left it there, cradling his head in his hand.

"What were you thinking, taunting him like that?"

How could I explain to him the demons that ran amok inside my head, the things that they whispered to me? I wasn't just in it for the adrenaline rush—I'd learned that early on—but there was something eerily intoxicating about being on the brink of death. It was euphoric, walking right up to death, and yet every time it spared me, as if hell didn't want me either.

I had stared down death many times in my life, more times than I should have for a woman of thirty-two. I knew from the trauma of my past that I'd been a messed up kid, and I'd only carried the weight of that into adulthood. The one time I had sought therapy in my young twenties, I had made the therapist cry, and that solidified my decision to never return. It wasn't like I could ever tell my therapist the truth behind the scars on my body or where the trauma truly came from.

There was no fixing me, just mending the broken pieces the best I could. How could I explain to my longest and most-trusted friend that I had a death wish, and I didn't know why? So, instead, I deflected the question with dark humor.

"The party needed some fresh entertainment." I shrugged apathetically, hoping he'd drop the subject.

"And the assassin, flying bullets, and now two dead body-guards weren't substantial enough for you?"

I bit my tongue, wanting to lash out at Dante, but he was loyal and I knew he meant well. He had been protecting not only me and my image, but also my assets for as long as I could remember. So, instead of reaming him out for simply doing his job, I avoided the interrogation entirely. My demeanor, however, quickly changed at the mention of my dead bodyguards.

"Please send compensation packages over to Ricardo and Miguel's families and let them know their burials will be paid for. I will meet with them soon to give my condolences as well," I stated, taking my heels off as I started to ascend the bronze 22k spiral staircase. I stopped halfway up the stairs, contemplating my next words, before I called back down to Dante, who was still standing there, silently agitated.

"Also, find out who that Matteo stranger was—the one that saved me—I'd like a formal introduction."

I didn't stay to gauge Dante's reaction to my request. Right now, all I wanted to do was strip out of this dress and soak in my oversized clawfoot tub and forget about the man with the dreamy forest green eyes that had been on the forefront of my mind for the last hour.

By the next evening, I had already paid my respects to Ricardo and Miguel's families and every time I held their wives' hands in my own, or saw their children huddled in the corner, wide-eyed, not fully registering that their dad was never coming home, I felt angry inside. I knew that feeling all too well, and it never got easier. My eyes glistened with unshed tears before I shook off the sorrow. I couldn't let them see me crumble.

"Never let them see your weaknesses," my father would always tell me.

I wasn't a fool. I knew I was dangerous. A vile monster that went bump in the night on the streets of Chicago. I had committed such atrocious acts, that even God himself would probably never forgive me. But, I did them so no one else had to. I took on that weight, so no one else had to bear witness to the unsavory things I had seen. The only reason I could sleep at night was knowing that anyone I had killed were bigger monsters than me and they had deserved it. Though I grew up in a religious family, my faith had somewhat wavered. I struggled to believe that there was someone up there who could forgive the atrocities I had committed. As a little girl, my father had made me pray every night, but as I got older I started to question my faith. If there was a higher power up there, why did my mother die giving birth to me? Why did my husband abuse me in such foul ways? Why was I held prisoner for five years? Was there such a thing as half-believing in a God? He would probably be judging me for my career choice.

But here in Chicago, I was the judge, jury, and executioner.

I hadn't always wanted this life. Deep down, I had a big heart that I had to lock away. One day came sooner than I imagined and I had to grow up, leave my childish, free-spirited heart behind. That little girl who believed in love was dead. Long gone.

Over the next two weeks, the stranger from the party with the captivating green eyes kept me up every night. When I closed my eyes, his face was there, and suddenly my mood got slightly better. I had been grieving the loss of my bodyguards —who were family to me—since the party, but tonight those haunting green eyes would once more be on me. I donned my black leather jacket and slipped on my Louboutins before I made my way down to the foyer, where Dante and two of my other men waited. Dante sported his aviator shades and just to rile him up, I took out my *Blowjob Red* lipstick and applied it to my lips using his shades as my mirror. Even though I couldn't see his golden-hued eyes, I could sense them rolling behind that barrier of his.

"What are we waiting for boys? Let's go."

I sauntered past them into the waiting vehicle just outside. I had a good feeling about tonight, and I tried to convince myself that it had nothing to do with the stranger Dante had finally hunted down.

CHAPTER FOUR

MATTEO

I WAS THREE DRINKS DEEP WHEN I HEARD THE DOOR OPEN TO the hole in the wall bar I found myself in.* I knew it wasn't just any random bar I had come across. It was in Emilia's territory, and one of the many businesses she owned. I knew from the way the bar faded of all noise and conversation that she had entered the room. I could've sworn even the faint hiss of the heat pumping through the room had held its breath momentarily.

I felt her presence behind me before I inhaled her scent, something warm and musky like settling in front of the fireplace on a cold winter day. I twirled my bourbon in my glass, keeping my back to her.

"If I didn't know any better, I'd think you were stalking me, *diavolessa.*"

Emilia stalked towards me like I was prey as she came around my side and sat down on the bar stool. I knocked back the rest of my glass as I peered over at her. She wore a slim-fitting leather jacket that went nicely with those leather pants she had on. I knew if she stood up they would look like they

---

* Devil Devil - MILCK

were painted onto her, and *god damn*, was I tempted to see what her ass would look like in those pants. They'd bring me to my knees in a heartbeat.

She wore a simple white tank underneath and when my eyes lifted to her face and met her ice-blue eyes, I felt my chest ignite. Tortured souls could write poetry about her eyes alone. They were so crystalline, they almost seemed translucent, absolutely breathtaking. My attention was drawn to her lips, her *cherry* red lips. I sent a prayer up to whoever pitied me at that moment for having to sit in front of this goddess, because all I saw when I closed my eyes was her on her knees, those luscious red lips swollen and bruised from me fucking her mouth. And then those lips started to move, and it took all of my concentration to focus on what she was saying.

"On the contrary, this is my bar. I should think you were the one that was stalking me, Matteo Ricci."

She signaled the bartender for two more drinks, and I didn't bat an eyelash that she had already dug into my past.

"First and last name basis, huh? Well, I'm honored you cared so much to do your homework on me."

It was then that the bartender dropped off our drinks before heading in the opposite direction to help another customer. I angled myself closer to her, as if we were two lovers having a private conversation.

"So, Miss DeLuca, what did your research say about me?"

She glanced up at me from the rim of her glass, and I watched as she drank the amber liquid, following its path down her throat. And for a brief moment, I felt jealous of the fucking glass pressed to her lips. Hell, even the bourbon as it trickled slowly down her throat. My thoughts went back to a certain body part wanting to find its home in the back of her throat, curious if she would gag.

"Your usual, ex-military stint to then playing the big bad contractor for whoever has the money to buy you for their services."

"And are you in need of my services?" I draw out the last word. I wasn't above flirting with her.

"Well, you see, I am down two bodyguards and that won't do."

"Hate to break it to you, sweetheart, but I'm only one man."

Her eyes trailed me from my feet all the way to my face, slowly and seductively, and I wasn't going to lie to myself about the fact that I enjoyed every second of it.

"Somehow I feel you are plenty of man for the job. This is not a permanent position, it's temporary only until I vet another person to take your place. I know you must be a busy man, what with all of your business dealings," she said with a flirtatious smile ghosting her lips.

I couldn't help but chuckle to myself at the ease with which she flirted back.

"Tell you what, sweetheart, I'll play you for it," I said, nodding over to the pool table behind her. "You win, I'll come work for you," I trailed off, making my way over to the pool table.

"And if I lose …?" she questioned, following me over, standing back while I rolled up my sleeves, racking the balls.

A smirk came across my face as I leaned over the table, cue stick in hand, my forearm flexing with the movement.

I bit my lip when I saw her eyes drop to my exposed fore-arms. I didn't want to reveal where my mind was taking me, but the devilish glint in her eyes tempted me to take her right there on that pool table.

"We'll save that for another time, *diavolessa*. Something tells me you're not a woman used to losing."

"You're right about that assumption."

And with that response from her, I sent the white ball flying across the felt table, all ten balls scattering every which way. Two solids hit their marks in their respective pockets.

When I lined up my next shot and sunk another ball, I beamed up at her.

"Maybe I spoke too soon. You may have some competition."

My last shot hit the ball at the wrong angle, and hit the side of the pocket before resting on the lip, teasing me.

"You were saying," she said with a cheeky grin.

She sauntered over to the side of the table where the cue ball had landed, her heels clicking across the cement floor. She dipped down, lining up her cue with the cue ball. And fuck me, I was already growing hard at those leather pants outlining all of Emilia's curves. I brought my whiskey to my lips, needing a distraction from the temptress in front of me.

My eyes studied her face, how her eyes squinted just slightly as she measured the angles, trying to find the perfect shot. Her teeth came down to bite her plush bottom lip, and I almost came in my pants right there like a teenager. She was a siren, this woman, and I was going to be in my own personal hell working for her. The clattering of balls striking tuned me back into focus just in time to watch the cue ball strike one of the striped balls, sending it forward to strike another one of her balls and simultaneously they sunk into two different pockets.

Damn, she was good.

I was going to work for her regardless; that was the overall mission, but I liked flirting with her, riling her up. Testing her.

"Game on," she smiled over at me, before she sunk another one of her balls in the back pocket. Her next ball just missed the pocket and pivoted towards the other end of the table.

I circled around the table towards her, where she remained rooted to the spot. When I took aim, figuring out my shot, she finally took a half-step back, but not before she slowly caressed my upper arm, dragging her bright red nails down its length. *This little minx,* I thought.

"How's your arm healing?" she asked, still drawing light circles on my bare skin, distracting me. I felt the goosebumps rise on my skin from her touch, and I saw out of the corner of my eye the ghost of a smile on her face as she saw the effect she had on me.

I smirked at her tactic, and just as I went to go make my shot, I felt the breath of her lips ever so delicately kiss where my wound was hidden beneath my shirt, and I botched the shot. We both watched the cue ball strike the eight ball and followed its path straight into the pocket.

"Looks like you're mine now," she said seductively into my ear.

I had no words for her. I was so turned on at the moment that I prayed that her and her guards didn't see the raging boner I was sporting in my jeans.

"I'll see you tomorrow," she waved over her shoulder, her Louboutins carrying her and that tantalizing scent of hers away. "Dante will send you the details."

I looked over to the exit, where I found Dante standing guard. He gave me a brief nod, and I dipped my chin back towards him. She paused at the door, hovering on the threshold next to Dante.

"Have a good night, Mr. Ricci."

There was a breeze in the night, there and then gone, and so was she.

I knew then I was fucked.

CHAPTER FIVE

EMILIA

I PICKED AT MY CUTICLE BEDS, A NERVOUS HABIT I'D NEVER kicked from when I was a child. If my father was still alive, he would've slapped my hands, scolding me that it wasn't a lady-like thing for me to do. He noticed small details like that—people's nervous tics—and he made sure I knew how to detect them. Being the Donna in the Italian mafia, these were things I'd had to ingrain into my mind and I was glad for that lesson. Noticing the nervous habits of others had saved my life multiple times in dicey situations. If there was one thing I trusted the most, it was my gut.

So, I knew it was hypocritical of me, as I picked the skin raw by my thumb, but I couldn't help the overwhelming feeling of anxiety crawling beneath my skin right now over the meeting I was about to walk into. After my masquerade party had ended abruptly and media outlets got wind of what had happened, I thought I had blown my initiation into the secret society, but they had reached out to me just as I was leaving my meeting with Matteo.

I was asked to come alone; no one in my organization had known about the invite I had received from the *Septem Daemonia*. I had heard rumors about this secret society running through Chicago at parties, and everyone had their suspicions of who may be part of the elite club, but they were just mere mumblings in the wind, no confirmations as of yet. Maybe I'd be the first to know. Since the party, I had been biding my time, and I was on edge. I pulled into the parking garage in my armored Mercedes G Wagon and made my way to the fifth level and parked. The entire fifth level was cleared of all cars, making it eerily quiet. I sat with the comfort of my 9MM in my lap as I waited tirelessly. Right at eleven, a blacked-out Escalade made its way toward my car and pulled up next to my driver's side door.

I rolled down my window half way, hiding my weapon. The other car did the same, and when the window rolled down to reveal a man in his fifties looking like your average Joe dad, it took all of my training to hide the shock on my face at the normalcy of his appearance.

"Miss DeLuca, it's a pleasure to meet you," the stranger stated calmly but with authority. "The *Septem Daemonia* welcomes you into their society," he continued.

I eyed the man curiously. I knew he wasn't a member of the secret society; I didn't think they'd show their faces, but he was definitely an employee of theirs. A negotiator or liaison of sorts.

"I haven't accepted the invitation just yet," I replied.

The man chuckles but carries on, "Well, they've done their research on you and they are impressed with your ambition and grit. The leadership you exude is exactly what they are looking for."

"They know all about your past and your present, and they see great things in your future. You bring prosperity and wealth back into Chicago, and the *Septem Daemonia* can help facilitate that even more. Your *businesses*," he emphasized, "can be even more profitable with the reach the *Septem Demonia* has. More profit, more power," he said with simple directness.

I thought for a brief moment before answering.

"And what percentage of the cut would the *Septem Daemonia* be taking for themselves?"

"Twenty percent of the profit. This also will guarantee you protection if needed, as the members are of a high status and have friends in high positions as well. You'd rule over Chicago like a true queen. The *Septem Daemonia* and you seem to have an enemy in common," he revealed, making me rear my head back in suspicion. Before I could ask for more details, given I had lots of enemies, the man had already slipped a business card through his window to me. I grabbed it quickly and pulled it into the safety of my car. It bore just a number, no name or address.

"Think about it, Miss DeLuca; the *Septem Daemonia* will be watching. When you are ready to accept, just call that number. Goodnight, Miss DeLuca."

And with that parting goodbye, the stranger rolled up his window, and drove off leaving me stunned and alone.

I didn't move an inch after the car had left. I knew it was dangerous being out in the open like this with my status, especially without backup I was an easy target for my enemies. The man had brought up that the secret society was well aware of my past, and I wondered if they knew all of it. Even the dark years, when I was off the grid for half a decade as a prisoner. I'd crawled my way to the top of where I was by the skin of my teeth and with my bare hands. In this world, women weren't handed anything like men were, especially the entire family business. I took it, earned it with blood and tears. My father didn't have any other children, so there was no son to hand over the keys to the kingdom of the DeLuca name, so he married me off to another Italian family in the business, only my father had underestimated just who he was selling me off too, and we had both paid the price for it. But, only one of them had lost their life over it.

I shuddered at the memory of those days. I was seventeen when I was married off to Romeo Morelli and those five years haunted me every time I closed my eyes. I'd tasted freedom for the first time at the ripe age of twenty-two. In the last ten years of my life, I'd reclaimed my right to the empire my father left behind and rebuilt it from the ground up. I'd earned the position I held, as it was rightfully mine for the taking. The DeLuca name was mine, and I would be damned if I let anyone take my title away from me. A name said everything about a person, and without it, I feared I'd be left with nothing.

The comfort of my 9MM still sat heavy in my lap as I forced myself back to reality. I slipped the weapon back into my holster at my hip and put the car into drive and made my way back to the compound, trying to enjoy the feeling of brief serenity before the nightmares would take me under once more as I slept. But the words of the stranger beckoned at me and ate away at my mind as I wondered who this common enemy we shared could be, and what it had to do with my possible initiation.

CHAPTER SIX

MATTEO

I was over this debrief with SSA Richards. The FBI thought they were running this operation, but it was never theirs to begin with. I zoned out during most of what the FBI agent was telling me since it wasn't anything I didn't already know. I had done my research on the DeLuca name, who Emilia was, and what I was up against. I didn't need the lecture.

"Emilia operates multiple businesses here in Chicago. All of them are legal entities and she's damn good at what she does, but we need proof of what goes on behind closed doors. These operations are legal fronts for her illegal dealings. We need a smoking gun," he demanded. "We need something to nail her to the wall."

"With all due respect, SSA Richards, I know how to do my job, and I do it well. Consider it done." I stood up, re-buttoning my tailored jacket as I go. "Now, if you'll excuse me, I need to meet with Emilia's second to acquaint myself with her ranks."

I didn't stay long enough to hear the mumbled answer from him, but I heard the distinct laugh of Tobias as I left the conference room. I strode down to the garage to my most prized possession in the world, my 1962 Ferrari 250 GTO. It was a rare commodity: only thirty-six were ever manufactured and they didn't come cheap. It shined bright red, a contrast to the dull gray and black sedans lined up in the FBI's underground garage. I didn't care much for anything; this car was my one and true love. Besides Tobias, I didn't have anyone else in my life. I turned the engine on, listening to the purr as I raced out of the car garage through the underground back tunnel.*

I flew through the streets of Chicago, pushing the car as fast as I could amongst other drivers. It was almost October, and fall was on the brink of coming through Chicago like a wave, but it was exceptionally warm today, so I rolled down all the windows and let the northern breeze keep me grounded. There was nothing like the rush of when I drove this car. In my head, I was already thinking about the next time I could take her to the open roads, open her up and let her run wild. When I was in those red leather seats, nothing else mattered. It was the only time I felt peace, even if it was only for a moment.

I didn't think about the mission that went to hell, or the brave men that were once friends of mine who had perished, or the mere fact that even though I was a powerful man myself with more money than I knew what to do with, I still felt utterly alone.

What should've been a twenty-minute drive to Emilia's compound in the heart of Lincoln Park took half the time. As I approached the wrought-iron gates and her guards let me through, I couldn't help but let out a resounding whistle at her wealth. I thought I was rich, but Emilia's wealth made me look like a beggar on the street. The style of her entire compound looked like it was plucked right from Italy itself and dropped here in Chicago. It was a true testament to

---

* I'm a Wanted Man - Royal Deluxe

classic European elegance and artistry. As I pulled up to the main entrance, Dante was already standing guard, waiting to greet me.

I stepped out of the car and buttoned my jacket as I made my way over to Dante. He shook my hand, but not before I saw Dante give my car a brief once-over, a look of envy flashing in his eyes. I smiled.

"Welcome. Let me show you around," Dante said with a curt nod, diving right into business.

I followed him through the big front doors, only to be left in complete awe of the interior. Emilia had truly brought home with her with the fine Italian cut marble, and the opulence of the front foyer was enough to leave anyone speechless.

I tuned in to everything Dante was telling me, making mental notes to myself as to where the other guards were stationed, and any and all exit points as Dante showed me where the kitchen, garage, and gym were located. It was when we had reached the professional level gym that I first caught a glimpse of Emilia since our run in at the bar. I still had fantasies of those leather pants and pouty red lips. Today, she was wearing tight black biker shorts that showed off her long, toned legs and a matching black sports bra that revealed a flat and chiseled stomach. She hadn't noticed us yet, as she was drying the sweat from her face. When the towel fell away, icy blue eyes pierced me to my core as our eyes locked and she smiled coyly at me. She wasn't wearing makeup, and she didn't need to. She was a goddess in the flesh, and for the second time that night I was left speechless.

"Matteo Ricci," she purred out my name like the siren she was, "pleasure seeing you again. I take it Dante has shown you the lay of the land."

She sauntered up to us, a hand on her hip and this close I could see the small beads of sweat dripping down her olive-toned skin into the valley of her cleavage, and I was tempted to follow its path with my tongue.

"Pleasure is all mine, Miss DeLuca. Thank you for welcoming me into your home. It's almost as stunning as its owner."

I was a flirt, and I didn't give two fucks that this was my new boss for the foreseeable future. That never stopped me from going after what I wanted, women included.

She smiled back at me.

"Thank you. I picked out everything myself down to every last detail."

Her eyes slid over to Dante, where it seemed like they were having their own conversation with their eyes.

"I'll escort Mr. Ricci to his room, Dante. I will see you later tonight though," she announced, dismissing him at the same time. He glanced back over at me as if he had words left unsaid, but instead turned back towards her and nodded, giving her a look of wariness.

She waited until Dante had left the room before she addressed me once more.

"How are you liking Chicago? I understand it's a long way from home for you," she said, trailing off at her own statement. We walked side by side out of her home gym, her taking the lead once we got to the end of the hallway.

"It's definitely a lot colder than it is back in California, but the temperate weather in San Francisco feels much like the current weather. Although I will admit I am not looking forward to a Chicago winter."

She smirked and eyed me skeptically when she stopped right outside the door.

"This is your room," she told me, waving towards a solid white door. "Dinner is at seven, and I expect you to be there every night on time, unless we have business," she mentioned, retreating backwards into what looked like her own room.

"I'll be there," I replied, watching every minute detail of her.

She turned her back to me, twisting the knob on her door, and I did the same with mine, but before I could step fully into my room, I heard her call out to me once more, and the next eight words out of her mouth, stopped me dead in the tracks, as she said each word with conviction.

"We both know I wasn't referring to California."

And with those parting words, she shut her door in my bewildered face.

CHAPTER SEVEN

MATTEO

It shouldn't have come off as a surprise to me that Emilia knew California wasn't home. It never would be either. My home was the same as Emilia's: Italy. No place in the world would compare to my home country. I grew up in northern Italy, in a town called Verona, or as the tourists liked to call it, the birthplace of the love of Romeo and Juliet. The romantics called it love, I called it a tragedy.

Though growing up in the north, I wasn't ignorant of what happened down in the western parts of Italy with the mafia families. I had heard of the DeLuca family once upon a time, until the name had disappeared off the face of the map, only to pop up years later in the United States.

I was born and raised in that city, and only left when my mother passed from cancer.

My father left when I was just a baby. While Italy had been my home for my whole life, it no longer felt like one with no family, so I left it behind.

I booked a flight as far as I could go in the United States and landed in the Bay Area looking to start fresh. I was twenty when I joined the United States Military. My military career became my entire life, and I ended up making a name for myself with the Navy Seals. With the Seals, I met Tobias and the rest of my team, or what was now left of it. If she knew where I had grown up, I wondered if she knew about what happened in Bolivia.When I had gotten out of the military and created my private security firm, I had erased my past, but with her resources, I didn't doubt that she could've easily found out my birthplace. But the mission in Bolivia, that was high-level security shit. She couldn't have access to that—could she?

I had to play my cards right with her. She was already proving to be a hard read for me. I had written her off as some pretty princess playing dress up with the big boys, but I had a feeling she would set me straight soon with my assumptions. A part of me was hoping for some entertainment.

I hopped in the shower, nothing but black stone and glass caging me in. I blasted the water and when it poured from the ceiling I let it scald my skin until I couldn't take it any longer, and I stepped out, wrapping a towel around my waist.

I threw on a pair of jeans and a black tee before making my way downstairs to the kitchen. It was almost seven, but everyone was already gathered around at the table. Most of her men were drinking beer at the long oak table, while Dante was surprisingly by the stove, hovering over a pan. I hadn't yet spotted Emilia.

As soon as I stepped into the kitchen, all conversation ceased and six heads swung towards me.

Dante was the one to speak first.

"Pull up a chair, Matteo. Dinner will be served shortly. Hope you like chicken parmigiana." His Italian accent was thick.

I nodded as Dante handed me a beer from the fridge.

"I see Emilia wasn't kidding about dinner being a mandatory thing, huh?" I asked Dante, popping off the top of my beer.

"Here, we are all *familia*. At the table, we are not cold-hearted killers but normal people enjoying a nice meal with friends. Emilia is big on making us feel like a family, and these dinners are important to her," he trailed off. "We still have matters to discuss," he quietly whispered under his breath. But, before I could reply, Emilia spoke up from behind me.

"We all take turns cooking, so I hope those genes of yours are good for something, *il mio cavaliere.*"

I turned to her and drank in her appearance. By the looks of it, she had showered not too long ago, because the ends of her hair were still damp. She wore leggings and an oversized sweater, large enough that she had to roll the sleeves back up to her elbows. *I wonder whose sweater it was.* Nowhere in my research did it mention a lover of sorts, but I had seen plenty of photos in the press of Emilia on the arms of some of the wealthiest and most good-looking men in Chicago, including Grant Ford, Chicago's widow tycoon.

She poured herself a generous glass of what looked like an expensive Cabernet and sat at the end of the table, jumping into the conversation her henchmen were having. She fit right in with them, and I could tell by their easy demeanor with her that they were comfortable around her as well. They respected her, which I found surprising. I didn't think that many men would take a woman in charge of an Italian mafia family lightly. I knew some probably hadn't, and that the seat she was in now hadn't been easy to reach.

I took a seat to the side of her, leaving the other side of her empty for Dante. It was at that moment that Dante brought over dinner: chicken parmigiana over linguini pasta and garlic bread. It smelled heavenly and for a minute I was thrown back into the past when I was a kid and my mother would cook this meal in our small apartment.

As I sat down, Emilia stood up and spoke.

"*Mi familia*, I cherish these moments with you. Our family dinners are special to me. No one can replace Miguel and Ricardo, and we will remember them always. There is a new

33

person at our table, and I'd like you to all welcome him, as he has earned a spot at this table. Matteo, welcome to the family. Saluti," Emilia cheered, raising her glass.

Her men followed suit.

And then I watched as six grown men launched themselves at the food, digging in. The silence at the table was riveting, watching these men gorge themselves on the homemade meal Dante had prepared, and I had to admit, it was one of the best chicken parmesan I'd ever had in my life, second to my mother's of course.

I sat back in my chair, sipping on my beer, and surveyed the dinner table. I knew the men at the table from my research. Sitting next to Dante was Enzo Veneziano, otherwise known as Lucky. He'd been a talented Formula 1 racer back in his youth, until a fiery accident almost cost him his life. It wasn't the first time he had avoided death's grip, hence the nickname. Sitting across from him at the table, I couldn't help but think he truly was one lucky son of a bitch. I remembered the news articles reporting his injuries saying it was touch and go for a bit and he would be in recovery for months, missing the entire season. It was an early retirement for him after that, and despite the burns that still flayed his hands and part of his arms, I could tell that Lucky missed the rush of the adrenaline and fast cars. When you're that young and everything you worked your whole life for gets ripped away from you, of course you'd miss it. I think it's why he chose to always drive. I think he secretly hoped for a high-speed chase.

Emilia recruited him soon after his hospital visit to come work for her, and he was the second one to fall in line behind her after Dante, who he was having a private conversation with right now. Lucky ran a hand over his well-kept beard, his brown eyes locked in on something Dante was showing him on his phone. I eyed him more closely, wondering if he too was looped into Dante's plan.

"So, Matteo, you're a *Frogman*, huh?" the man next to me

asked. I turned in my seat and took him in. He had dark hair that I could best describe as luscious, and it just grazed the tops of his shoulders. I racked my brain for his name, my memory coming back with the name Stefan Esposito. Emilia's sharpshooter, he was the one they called Ace and was the best of his kind on his team, so much so that his name was tossed around a lot all the way out in California. He was originally from Brooklyn, the East Coast version of Tobias and his biggest competition. I had heard about his last mission and how he had been hit. I was shocked that the bullet hadn't done more damage. The bullet had merely grazed his head, and only left him with a scar above his left eyebrow. I wondered if that was why he grew his hair a bit longer, to cover up the scar.

"I was, yes, out in California. I hear you crushed it out over on the East Coast. We joked about your skills to our friend, as to who would win in a competition," I replied. "We fucked with him a lot about you kicking his ass if you two were ever to meet."

Stefan reared his head back laughing, and from the corner of my eye, I saw Emilia lose interest in her conversation with Dante, and glance my way.

"I rained down hell over there." Stefan beamed proudly. "They sent us over to Belgrade for a bit." He absentmindedly started to rub his scar as he spoke about that place. He didn't elaborate more on Serbia, but I recognized the haunted look that crossed his face. His eyes glazed over, and I would bet my entire life's work that he was remembering that exact moment the bullet made impact.

Navy Seals were the best of the best, the strongest and most courageous. But they were also the craziest bastards you'd ever meet. I felt a kindred spirit in Stefan. Hell, I might even grow to like him.

I gave him a quick squeeze on his shoulder, and he looked up and gave me a small smile in return. As I reached for my beer once more, I felt the eyes of Emilia on me, and when I looked up, she was openly watching me, drinking in the details. I couldn't quite place the look on her face, but it almost resembled something like warmth.

Dinner continued, conversations carrying across the long table. I caught quips and jabs as they roasted one another and chattered about the latest women they were with, and I committed it all to memory, grasping for a crumb of information about Emilia's dealings.

"So, does this make me the seventh dwarf in this family fairy tale of yours?" I whispered over into Emilia's ear. As I did so, I could smell the essence of her, the coconut body wash scent filling my senses.

"Dwarf?" she questioned. Her eyebrows dipped, and she had the cutest scrunch right in between. I ran my thumb over the spot delicately, smoothing it out. I realized what I had done too late, when I heard Dante clear his throat in the background. I quickly snatched my hand back, internally chastising myself. *What was it about her that drew me in?* I felt this invisible pull toward her, like I was tethered to her despite not knowing much about her other than mere facts. She truly was a siren, and being in her presence, I couldn't help but fall under her song.

She broke me out of my inner scolding as a quiet laugh escaped her.

"I don't think they would prefer to be called dwarves, huntsmen seems more like their style."

I gave her a quick smile and returned to my meal. Dinner went on seamlessly after that, and I kept to myself for the most part, nodding my head and making barely audible grunts when needed. Eventually, after dinner wrapped up and dessert was served, Emilia's men slowly started to turn in for the night or to venture off into the city.

"You're on cleaning duty," Dante stated, pointing at me as he turned and walked out of the room.

I started to stack the remaining dishes and carried them over to the sink. I washed each dish meticulously, and I felt her rather than heard her approach. She picked up the dishes I'd washed laying on the counter and started to hand dry them. Neither of us said a word, as we were simply content standing there, working in silence. When the dishes were done, we put them away and Emilia started to turn off the lights.

I quietly mumbled a good night to Emilia and turned to head back to my room. Just as my hand touched the edge of the banister, she spoke softly in the darkness behind me.

"You'd be Bashful."

I heard her retreating footfalls, and it wasn't until I was halfway up the stairs that I realized she had been referring to my earlier question. I may come off as shy around her and her men, but sweet I was not, and sooner or later she would know that too.

CHAPTER EIGHT

EMILIA

*I SPENT THE NEXT MONTH IN MEETINGS OR HIDDEN AWAY IN the gym, sweating out my frustration. If I wasn't stressing about my decision with the secret society and keeping it a secret from my second, I was growing agitated with all the fantasies my mind concocted of Matteo. Having him mere feet from my bedroom door was not helping at all. He appeared in my dreams and every morning when I woke up, I was filled with so many pent up feelings, that I found myself slipping my hand underneath my sheets. I had to bite down hard on my lip to keep from moaning out his name, for fear of him happening to overhear it.

Hitting punching bags in my gym seemed to be a better form of getting out all my frustration, but it just didn't have the same rewarding feeling. To my horrifying recollection, it had been just over a year since I was intimate with someone. He'd been a broker for the wealthiest elite and in Chicago on business until the project was concluded, so for two months I'd slipped into his bed and left before the sun rose. He was more than okay with our little arrangement, as was I.

---

* Dirty Thoughts - Chloe Adams

I didn't want a relationship, just someone who could take care of my needs, and he'd done a decent job, but more times than not, I still found myself getting off after. And I didn't dare cross the line with any of my men. Not for lack of interest; they were all quite good looking and I knew if I had put the offer on the table for any of them, they'd be more than willing, but I never wanted to mix the two. Growing up my father had always told me not to shit where I eat, and I never had. I'd kept pleasure separate from work, until now. Now, I was conflicted. Matteo was only working under me temporarily until I found a replacement. It was that technicality alone that made me not feel half as guilty of getting off to the image of Matteo.

My head fell back in a wordless scream as my orgasm hit me like a tsunami. My fingers kept working at my clit as I rode out my high, my inner thighs slick with the mess I'd made. I was panting by the end, my hand grasping the sheets underneath me. I headed to the bathroom to clean myself off, only feeling slightly less unhinged.*

After rinsing off in the shower briefly, I swiped the condensation off my bathroom mirror, taking in my rosy cheeks. The water from my hair dripped down my flushed skin, as I stepped into my bedroom bare. Call me conceited, but I loved being naked. I worked hard for the body I had, and if I could I'd flaunt it every day. Despite my past and what I had experienced, I craved the attention of men and women. When all eyes were on me, I felt powerful. I knew when men looked at me, they saw my curves and a pretty face and not the woman beneath the surface, women too, and that was fine. I liked being looked at as if they wanted to devour me. I knew I turned heads when I walked into a room, usually due to my reputation or because of my looks, and I didn't mind either one. I let my hair dry naturally, liking the way it curled when I

---

* Stop playing Dirty Thoughts - Chloe Adams

did, and expertly applied my makeup in the mirror. I made sure the wing of my eyeliner was extra sharp today.

I donned an olive green suit jacket that dipped low in the front and paired it with slim fitting pants that hugged my frame and were tight by my ankles. I decided to forgo anything underneath my jacket, making the choice to be a little risque today. I sat on my bed, bending over to throw on my Louboutins, when there was a curt knock on my door. I voiced for them to come in, and was met with dark, expensive Prada shoes in my line of vision. I lifted my head halfway to find a devilishly handsome Matteo standing before me.

"Allow me, *diavolessa*," he purred, as he knelt between my open legs and slipped my shoe on my foot. My heel now rested lightly on his chest, the material stretching underneath, defining every detail that lay below. He was ripped, and it showed, and I was blatantly staring.

I snapped out of my stupor, and allowed myself to sneak a peek at his face, where I found a dazzling smirk.

"Do you always go above and beyond for your clients?" I teased.

"Only the beautiful ones," he quickly countered, the bare graze of his fingertips coasting over my ankle, drawing a shiver from my body. He smiled up at me then, his eyes narrowed into slits as he assessed my top and the cleavage that was showing. His fingers lingered briefly on my skin as he cleared his throat multiple times, knowing the effect I had on him, as he slowly lowered my foot back to the ground.

He offered me his hand and I took it, standing up. Even in my three inch heels, I was still a couple inches short. My eyes fell just at eye level of his Adams apple. My mind wandered back to earlier in the shower, where I had fantasized about placing wet kisses in that area, and I loudly cleared my throat, feeling dazed.

I kept my hands busy, by applying my *Blowjob Red* lipstick to my full lips, making a smacking sound as I finished. I grabbed my phone on my nightstand, and turned towards the door, where Matteo stood, committing every detail of me.

As I strutted past him, I swore I saw his eyes dilate and darken in desire, but I could've been mistaken. He was a beautiful distraction, and one I could not let myself have. I was not a woman who mixed business with pleasure, but I found myself making excuses each time as to why Matteo would be good for me. The number one reason being I needed to get laid.

Lucky drove us today in their armored SUV, Dante sitting in the front seat, vigilant as always, and I was in the backseat, Matteo to my left. I was meeting with one of my associates over in Lincoln Square. We parked just outside Davis Theater, entering through the back way, Lucky staying outside in the lobby, while Dante and Matteo followed me inside to theater two. My heels clicked on the sticky linoleum stairs as I made my way to the top, where my contact, *La Rana*, waited. They called him the Fisherman because his business specialized in "transportation of goods and products" and his preferred form of transportation was shipping containers. He moved goods fast and efficiently, and it helped that he was the commanding officer of Chicago's docks. Nothing came in or out of the port without his knowledge.

I took a seat in the row behind him, my eyes taking in everything around me. There was no movie playing on the screen, so we were the only ones in the room.

"Miss DeLuca, your shipment has arrived and is ready for pickup. We have a new guard on rotation, so I would suggest a time frame no earlier than 1 am," he reported, pulling his hat lower on his head.

"Noted," I answered, extending an envelope of cash in between the armchairs. He took it from me discreetly, pocketing it inside his suit jacket, tapping it once.

"And the other thing I had you look into for me?"*

"There's word about a shipment coming in three weeks' time with the unmentionables you inquired about. Shall I stop it from entering?"

"No," I replied curtly. "Let it through, I'll take care of the rest," I said firmly, standing up and making my way back down the stairs.

I passed by Dante and Matteo standing guard and they filed into the lobby where Lucky was. Dante nodded to him, and he exited before us, his head rocking side to side to check for threats. He had already crossed the street and filed into the driver's side when the rest of us exited the building. I was just crossing the street, Matteo at my side and Dante at my six, when I heard the engine turn over three times, stalling at each turn. My eyes widened in horror, and I screamed Lucky's name but he didn't hear me. He attempted to start the car once more, and as he did the car exploded, flames engulfing the entire vehicle. The force of the explosion threw me off balance, and as the car exploded into flying pieces of metal, I hit the asphalt hard, my head hitting the pavement. And everything went black.

---

* Up in Flames - Ruelle

CHAPTER NINE

EMILIA

I woke up confused and sore in the comfort of my bed back at the estate. I slowly opened my eyes, visions of what happened coming to the forefront of my mind. The car engine stalling. Me screaming Lucky's name, to no avail. The burst of light blinding me as the car engulfed my friend in a fiery blaze. The color gray as I hit the ground, and then nothing.

I struggled to sit up in bed until Dante slowly edged me back to a lying position.

"Easy, Emmy," he told me, concern laced in his voice. I faintly heard him call for our doctor. It paid to have doctors in your pocket. Can't exactly walk into a hospital with a gunshot or stab wound without them reporting it to the police.

It was only myself and Dante in the room.

"How long have I been out?" I asked hoarsely, my lips parched and dry.

"Five hours," he quipped, agitated more over the situation than my question.

"You were close to the car when the bomb went off. The doctor said you have a mild concussion, but no fractures, luckily. And you have a few bruised ribs, which will be sore for a few weeks. Scans came back negative for any internal bleeding. You escaped with only some superficial cuts along your face."

I grimaced at that last part, and he caught it and coughed out a small laugh.

"Nothing that a few days won't heal. You won't even have a scar, promise."

"Who was it?" I demanded of him.

Dante perched on the edge of my bed, his hands making a mess of his hair.

"We don't know. I sent Matteo out to scan the surrounding area for any clues. Adrian hasn't stopped sifting through cameras in a five-mile radius of the place, but no word yet," he sighed, defeated.

"I want them dead and for it to be a slow and painful death," I seethed, blind rage coursing through me. I could feel my heart racing, thinking about how I would torture the person responsible for taking Lucky's life. He was still a young kid, only twenty-six. He'd been nineteen when he met me. He'd had so much potential, so much life to live. Death had come for me and he was the casualty of my war. Another grave I would have to dig. Another unanswered prayer for redemption. It came full circle, Lucky and I. I had met him the day his race car caught on fire, and today a fiery blaze took him anyway, just seven years later. Karma truly was a vicious cunt.

"We can't lose anyone else, Dante," I said as tears crested in my eyes at the loss of another family member.

Dante's golden eyes pierced mine as he promised retribution.

"We won't. That I can promise you. Whoever did this will know no mercy."

My life flashed before my eyes today. One second I was watching Emilia scream frantically, running toward the vehicle, toward danger, and the next, she was thrown through the air, her body coming down hard on the pavement. We wouldn't have been able to save Lucky, but I wished that I could've. Even if only for her, seeing how devastated she was to lose someone close to her. I would cleave through space and time if I could rewind this day and prevent it from happening. But I couldn't. So, once the doctor had sedated her and cleared her of any major injuries, I'd jumped into my car and dialed Tobias immediately, telling him to meet me near Millenium Park. *I punched the gas, racing toward what I hoped would be answers.

I came face to face with myself as I stared into the reflection of the steel structure before me. Chicago's skyline rested behind me, the sky painted a glowing orange. There were many things I felt as I stared at the man in the reflection: hollow, a failure, a ghost. I didn't have time to reflect on these thoughts, as I saw Tobias walking toward me. He stood next to me, about ten feet apart, pretending to be engrossed in the structure before us.

"Who set the bomb to kill Emilia?" I led with, withholding small talk.

He followed my lead and cut to the chase.

"Have you ever heard of *La Corredora*?"

---

*   Up in Flames - Ruelle

My head whipped in Tobias's direction, a flash of fear in my eyes.

"What does the leader of Mexico's most dangerous and lethal drug cartel have anything to do with the bomb that took out one of Emilia's men? That dirty bomb was meant for her," I snapped.

Tobias looked at me questioningly. "And you, brother. You're her bodyguard now. That easily could have been you."

"I'm not concerned about my safety. I've seen and been through worse."

We made eye contact; a silent beat passed between us as we both remembered our military days.

I repeated my question, and Tobias sighed loudly before answering me.

"*La Corredora's* hitman planted the bomb. The FBI confirmed it. It's her."

I shook my head, confused.

"Why would she attack Emilia and her men? It doesn't add up. *La Corredora* deals in cocaine and human trafficking, Emilia doesn't deal with either of those. This wouldn't be a turf war, so why make the hit?" I questioned, hoping Tobias would have the answer. "What's the connection? Do you think it's personal? I don't think Emilia would deal in human trafficking."

"I wish I could tell you, but that's all the information I have. You need to get closer to her, Matteo. Whatever it takes."

I nodded, silently agreeing. I turned to head back to my car, when Tobias spoke up again, facing his reflection in the structure.

"Quickly, Matteo, otherwise there is going to be a war here in Chicago and many innocent people are going to get hurt."

I didn't need to respond. I knew what I had to do; I had

always known. But my gut wrenched at the thought of it. She would never forgive me, and it was that thought alone that kept me distracted the entire drive back to her.

CHAPTER TEN

MATTEO

After a week, Emilia insisted on getting out of bed, despite the doctor's warnings about giving her head time to heal from the concussion. If there was anything I had quickly learned about Emilia, it was that she was a stubborn woman with an attitude on her. And she could be very persistent.

Dante and I had decided to switch up the vehicles and routes after Lucky's murder, and put our driving routes on a random rotation, so if *La Corredora* was watching her every move, Emilia would be harder to track. It was my idea to also have a decoy car leave first from the compound, in case anyone was tailing her, and then the car with Emilia actually in it would leave fifteen minutes after the first.

After my conversation with Tobias last night, I rushed back to Emilia's, only to find her passed out in bed, a slight snore echoing throughout her room. I didn't know how long I had been there staring at her, when Dante gripped my shoulder and beckoned me to follow him outside quietly.

"What did you find out?"

I filled him in on what I could tell him. Told him I had my tech guy back at my company tap into the FBI's database and that the dirty bomb on Emilia's car was put there by a

Mexican drug cartel. When I mentioned the name of it, his face went white as a sheet, and I knew my answer then. Dante wouldn't elaborate on the situation, but somehow Emilia was enemy number one to them, and I was determined to find out why that was.

Four days later, I watched Emilia hold Lucky's grieving mother in her arms, a stark contrast as to what the rest of the city assumed and believed of Emilia's character. I couldn't exactly defend her—I knew the horrors she had committed—but yet, I couldn't judge her either. I was the same. But from what I had gathered thus far, this Emilia before me was another side of her that she didn't let most people see. I could tell that she truly cared for her men. To her, they didn't just work for her and keep her safe, they truly were her family. And when a family member was slain in this line of work, you got revenge. And she was on the warpath for blood to be spilled.

She sat there holding her, Emilia's hands running through his mother's hair as she offered her condolences. I stood by the front door of Lucky's mother's residence, my head on a constant swivel. It had been a risk coming here, being exposed like this, but Emilia had been insistent that this was something she needed to do. After another hour of Emilia sipping coffee with Lucky's mother, we made our way back to her residence, where she slipped back into her bedroom, shutting the door.

I retreated to my room where I pulled out my laptop, hoping to dive into more background research on what Emilia's connection was to *La Corredora*, but from the ages of seventeen to twenty-two, Emilia was a ghost. The last information I had about her was her being married off to Romeo Morelli, another huge name in the Italian mafia. On her twenty-second birthday, July 28th, she had made headlines once more as she came back to the world with no husband and a vengeance to regain her family name. But that five year gap left me with so many questions.

Was this when she'd had contact with La Corredora?

I spiraled down a rabbit hole trying to put the missing puzzle pieces together, only to wind up nowhere. Even my most trusted and talented hacker couldn't find anything on Emilia in her missing years. If anyone knew where she'd been, it had to be Dante. But, there wasn't much I could do at the moment, so I decided a quick workout might suffice and quiet the voices inside my head. I threw on some track pants and laced up my shoes before heading down to the gym. And once again, I found myself alone with Emilia.*

She hadn't noticed me yet. She was too preoccupied with the punching bag in front of her. She wore tight black leggings and a cropped tank top. I could see the sweat glistening off her skin from the doorway, and I wondered just how long she had been here for. The bruises on her ribs were a sickly yellow, but if she was in any kind of pain, she didn't reveal it. I'm sure she'd had worse injuries than this, given her line of work.

"Might be better to practice on a moving target," I mentioned out loud, letting her know I was there. "If you'd like," I followed up.

She threw another punch, before she grabbed the bag to stop its momentum and turned towards me.

She shrugged her shoulders as she replied to me.

"Been awhile since someone has offered to be my human punching bag."

---

* Dangerous - Sleep Token | Spotify Playlist

I laughed. "Sweetheart, I offered to be your sparring partner, not your punching bag."

"They're one and the same, are they not?" she jested.

"Touche, darling. Guess we will find out soon enough," I quipped back, readying myself to fight with her. I wasn't sure what to expect with Emilia, but I knew she wasn't going to hold back. She came charging at me full force, but I was ready for her. I was trained by the Navy Seals, and while learning how to fight was a tool we all had to know to survive, she'd grown up fighting as a *way* to survive.

She was scrappy, but her moves were precise. They would've done damage, that was a given fact, if I had not blocked them. She kept her guard up; not once did she allow her hands to drop from position. She'd been on the attack, so I decided to switch up my game, see how she was when she was on the defensive. I threw a right hook to her face, and she leaned back, dodging the hit, right as I threw another one her way from the opposite side, but she was quick to recover and duck down and out of the way. Next thing I knew, a front kick came flying into my chest, throwing me off balance and away from her. Just as I was about to take a step toward her, her entire body came barreling at me, all 5'6" of her, as her left leg made contact with my stomach, a powerful blow. It happened in a split second. I didn't even see it coming. After her blow to my stomach, she had both legs wrapped around my head, her body twisting in the air, as she brought me down for the takedown.

I only had two thoughts after.

She did not just use a flying head scissor on me like this was an Avengers movie.

And *I'm going to marry this woman.*

She quickly flipped herself around to straddle me, her feet slipping under my legs to lock them in, while simultaneously pinning my hands down by my ears, and I was fucking beyond impressed with this woman. Her sleek midnight-hued hair cascaded down around us like a waterfall, and I smirked up at her, right as I flipped us, so she was the one pinned to the mat.

"Is this why they call you the *Black Widow*?" I asked, lowering myself to whisper into her ear. Her chest was heaving from our sparring, and I couldn't help but get lost in the sweat pooling down her neck, my eyes tracing its path down into her cleavage.

As I looked back up into her eyes, I saw that they were filled with mischief and desire.

Our mouths were so close to touching that when she exhaled, I inhaled, sharing breaths.

She leaned forward, her response at the edge of my lips as she whispered, "They call me the *Black Widow* because they believe I killed my husband."

Nothing about this conversation should be turning me on, but the feeling of having Emilia underneath me like this had me on edge and I was seconds away from falling. She smiled seductively up at me, sensing my bulge getting bigger between her legs.

I ignored my body, betraying me like I was a teenager getting a hard on for the first time.

"And did you? Kill your husband?"

I don't know why I asked her. Even if she had, I'm not sure I would even care.

She cocked her head to the side.

"A lady never reveals her secrets."

I stared at her for so long, trying to find the meaning behind those words. A part of me knew the answer was yes. As for the reasoning, that's what piqued my curiosity. But before I could question her further, a throat cleared behind us. Whatever moment that was happening between us dissipated.

"You should probably get ready for the gala; it starts in less than two hours," Dante called over to us from the doorway. I climbed to my feet, extending my hand out to Emilia. She took it, and the electric current that coursed through my body almost brought me to my knees. Her small gasp told me she felt it, too. Ten seconds passed and neither of us looked away, our hands still interlocked. Eventually, she broke the tension seeping off of us, and right as she walked by me, she placed her hand over my chest, her hand sliding dangerously low, but never quite getting to where I wanted it to land. Instead, she stopped right above the waistband of my pants.

"You may want to take care of that before the event," she suggested, before I watched her retreat from the room. I didn't know what had transpired in this last half hour, but all I knew was she had me intrigued to know every layer of her.

CHAPTER ELEVEN

MATTEO

DANTE STOOD OVER BY THE DOORWAY, WATCHING ME suspiciously as Emilia bent over to grab her towel that had been left off to the side of the mat. I didn't dare take my eyes off of him, because I wouldn't put it past him to put a bullet in me if he caught me staring at her ass. I kept my eyes straight ahead as Emilia started to walk past him, and he reached out to grab her arm and whisper something in her ear. Her eyes quickly glanced back my way before she nodded at Dante and walked out of the room.

I headed over to the punching bag, not yet ready to leave this room until I had exhausted all my energy. I felt Dante hovering behind me as I laid into the punching bag.

"What do you think you are doing?" he demanded.

I didn't bother turning around as I took my anger and feelings out on the bag before me. The bag shook from side to side with every hit I threw. I could feel the ache in my arms, but I didn't dare stop.

"My job," I answered, unfazed by his interrogation of my intentions with Emilia.

"That's not the job we discussed. I hired you to get intel from the FBI, not to crawl your way into Emilia's sheets. Stick to the plan before you make me regret my decision to have you here," he said with conviction, his eyes darting around nervously.

He didn't wait for my response before leaving the room. I screamed out into the void before I put all of my strength into one last hit on the bag, sinking to the floor in defeat.

Emilia joined me in the foyer an hour later. I watched as she descended the staircase, her heels clicking on the marble. Her satin crimson-colored dress flowed behind her like a river of blood in her wake, her toned leg peeking out from the thigh-high slit with every step she took toward me. She was absolutely timeless and elegant. The neckline dipped low, drawing my attention to her high, full breasts as they teased the eye. There was delicate beading on the neckline, enhancing her figure even more, and off-the-shoulder straps fell down her arms, adding an elegant touch to it. I was left in complete awe at the woman that stood before me.

"*Diavolessa* indeed," I whispered, licking my lips. My eyes lingered on her figure in that dress as I swept her hand up in mine, gently brushing a kiss to the top of her hand.

"And are you ready to dance with the devil?" she purred back to me.

I drank her in. Her dark hair was pulled back into a tight ponytail, the waves of it falling over her spine. If she asked me to, I would fall to my knees and worship her. She'd become my new religion.

"I'm willing to commit whatever sin you'd ask me to." I found myself confessing, and I was not even shocked at the truth behind those words. I *would* commit whatever sin she told me to.

She eyed me, her lips tilting up. "Be careful what you wish for, Mr. Ricci."

I looped my arm through hers as I guided her over to my car and opened the door for her.

"Your chariot," I said, gaining a laugh from her.

I circled around the back of my car and watched through the rear window as she took in my car, admiring it while I shamelessly admired her. As I settled into my seat and revved the engine, I waited for her other bodyguards to take their positions and we drove in separate directions, the plan to meet up at the fundraiser. No one would suspect Emilia in my car as opposed to one of her armored, blacked-out vehicles.I was beyond happy with the situation because I wanted more time with her, more time to get to know her.

I peeled out of the gate and took off down the street, heading south toward the harbor where Grant Ford was hosting his annual Chicago Angels Project Gala. This year, he was hosting it at the Art Institute of Chicago, one of the oldest museums in the country, where the venue space itself boasted elegance and vintage glamour. And tonight it fell on Halloween. I had heard about Grant Ford in passing. He was amongst Chicago's upper class, and it didn't surprise me in the slightest that he and Emilia had been an item of sorts at some point. He was an entrepreneur who owned luxury hotels and Michelin star restaurants all over the globe, along with a tech company and Chicago's one and only casino. He was a billionaire, good-looking and a charmer, and women fawned over him. But he was passionate about this project of his, with all proceeds going to breast cancer research, and he vowed every year to match everyone's donations.

It was only a fifteen-minute drive to the fundraiser, but I

took my time driving there. It was a crisp October night, and it was a beautiful evening to have the windows down. Emilia's ponytail blew in the autumn breeze and I found myself drawn to her like a moth to a flame. When she thought no one was looking, she wore a carefree smile, and her red dress made her blue eyes more vibrant.

"What's your favorite color?" I found myself randomly asking her.

She peered over at me, her eyebrows crinkled, and I found it amusing and cute on her.

"I've never really thought about it," she eventually answered. She peered down at the giant emerald ring on her middle finger, and leaned back into her seat. She started to twirl the ring as she looked back over at me and continued, "I guess I would say green. Anytime I felt that my life was chaotic, I would look at this ring and ..." She trailed off as if she didn't want to finish.

"And what?" I prodded, glancing over at her.

She dropped her eyes, as if embarrassed.

"And it would bring me peace. Like its presence would drench me in calm. I clung to that feeling in dark times as a reminder that there was light at the end of the tunnel. It's silly I know."

I didn't know what possessed me, but I reached over and grabbed her hand in her lap, my head leaning close to hers.

"It's not silly at all," I addressed her fully as we stopped at a red light. I didn't take my eyes off her as I spoke.

She forcibly swallowed, as her head fell dangerously close to mine, her eyes darting back and forth between my eyes and my lips. I started to lean in closer to kiss her, like I thought she wanted me to, when the car behind me honked their horn at the now green light ahead of us. I jumped back to my side of the car and stepped on the gas as she cleared her throat and asked me the same question, shifting in her seat, one leg crossing over the other.

I drew circles into her hand, still clasped in mine. Without taking my eyes off of her, I looked deeply into hers and said the only thing that would forever haunt me even after I was gone.

"Blue."

CHAPTER TWELVE

EMILIA

I HADN'T FELT LIKE MYSELF LATELY, NOT SINCE THE EXPLOSION, and it wasn't because of my injuries. Half of it was due to losing Lucky, and the other was due to Dante informing me of who was behind the attack. *La Corredora* was bringing the war to my front doorstep, and she wanted me to know. I thought I had escaped that part of my life. I had dug my way out, spilled blood for my freedom. I'd clawed my way back to life after near death. I'd turned a life full of pain and misery into power. Chicago was *my* city, *my* home. I was the queen here, and I didn't bow to anyone's commands.

Matteo and I didn't run into any issues on the drive, and for a brief time I felt normal. He asked me what my favorite color was, and it threw me off, because up until a few minutes ago I didn't think I had one, and I feel like that's an odd thing, to not have a favorite color. I hadn't thought much about it, until I looked down at my emerald ring my father had given me as a wedding present. It had been one of his last gifts to me before his execution at the hands of my ex-husband. I'd found out about his death a year later, after my husband at the time had grown tired of me and sold me off to the highest bidder. I'd held onto that ring, even when some forcefully tried to remove it. It was the one thing I had left to remember him by.

The smell of bergamot and leather filled my nose and brought me back into the present, as I took in Matteo hovering over me, his hand extended. I took his offered hand and exited his car, following him up the steps into the main area where a friend of mine was hosting his fundraiser gala. The heart of the space was flooded with pink uplighting, white tablecloth linens draped to the floor, and pink napkins and tapered candles donned the tables. Champagne flutes floated throughout the room on trays held by waitstaff, the women dressed in pink dresses and heels, while the men wore pink ties with their suits. Grant always hosted parties throughout the year, but this fundraiser was his pride and joy. We made our way through the crowd over to where Dante and the rest of my security team stood on high alert. I gave them a brief nod before turning and saying hello to the host.

"Emilia, darling, what an absolute stunner you are tonight," he said, twirling me around in a circle. "Thankfully, this event is about breasts, and not hearts because you would give half of these men a heart attack."

"Who says I still won't?" I lightly tease back.

He leaned in, our bodies almost flush. "Still won't give me a chance, huh?" he whispered half-teasingly.

I shook my head at him before answering him. "You know why I can't," I said with a little regret in my voice. "Plus you couldn't handle a woman like me," I teased, trying to lighten the tension. We had gone on a few dates in the past, and he was a wonderful lover, but first and foremost he was a father, and I was the furthest thing from what Grant needed around his daughter. I'd only bring danger to their lives, and he was kind and didn't deserve that kind of life at his doorstep.

I smiled kindly over at him, before picking up the paddle for the silent auction later.

"See you out there, Grant."

"Save me a dance, will you?" he called out to me with a smile before heading back into the crowd surrounding him.

I responded with a nod before heading over to the bar where I ordered myself a whiskey neat and looked out over the crowd. Powerful men in suits cozied up to other wealthy men, and influential women worked the room, ears to the floor for the latest news. I sighed at the fact that these parties were always the same. Most of them just showed up for the party and threw cash at whatever they were supporting, without actually bothering to do anything more to help. I didn't want to run my city this way, which is why I took a more hands-on approach with stuff that mattered to me. That was one of the many reasons why I had befriended Grant in the first place. He too had a very hands-on approach to things he was passionate about.

Grant's voice echoed throughout the room from the head of the stairs as he addressed those who had attended.

"Ladies and gentleman, it pleases me that so many of you came out to support me and my cause. This project of mine turned into a passion for me in the last five years, as you all know. Five years ago, I lost my late wife, Alessandra, to breast cancer and it has been a long journey since. I started this Angels Project as a way to help find a cure, to detect this cancer gene quicker. I didn't have as much time as I had hoped I would with my wife, but in her last year with me, she gave me the greatest blessing, my daughter Avery. Your proceeds tonight will go towards aiding in the extensive research as well as helping these families pay for treatments while they cope with their new reality. I thank you from the bottom of my heart for your generous donations. So, dig deep into those pockets tonight, folks." He laughs, before turning away from the mic and stepping into the crowd.

It was nearing the end of Grant's fundraiser, and after two whiskeys and writing out a check for $25,000 to go toward his Angels Project, I was about ready to take my heels off and soak in my nice clawfoot tub. I downed the rest of my drink before I grabbed my clutch and started to make my way through the swarm of drunk people heading towards the women's bathroom. It was when I was washing my hands that I noticed the bathroom had cleared out quickly and my gut screamed at me to look up. As I did, a wire was thrown around my neck, cutting off my circulation by a man bearing two tattooed blood drops on the side of his head—a mark I'd recognize anywhere. The mark of *La Corredora's* cartel. I saw my eyes go wide in the mirror. This wasn't how I was going to go out. With all my strength, I brought one of my legs up, dug my heel into the countertop, and pushed off, slamming the man back into the wall. His hands gripped me, tearing my dress. I bent low at the hip, swinging my assailant's body over me onto the bathroom floor, where I wasted no time sliding my dagger across his neck, just as the bathroom door swung open and Matteo came flying in, clothes disheveled, as if he'd raced through the crowd of people to get to me.

"Don't worry, I got it," I mustered, my voice barely above a whisper, as I doubled over, trying to catch my breath. I gripped my stomach with one arm and stood up, leaning against the bathroom sink for support. I looked at myself in the mirror and caught Matteo's face in the reflection. His pupils were blown out and the green of his irises had darkened two shades as his eyes followed the trickle of blood crawling its way down my neck.

"You're bleeding," he growled.

"Thanks for stating the obvious, but I'll be fine," I managed to croak out. The pressure the assassin had put on my windpipe was damaging enough that he had definitely bruised it, making my voice come out hoarse and raspy. "Can't seem to say the same thing for him," I shrugged, turning around.

*Matteo's gaze consumed me, as his eyes traveled from my feet, where one of my shoes came off in the scuffle, to the slit in my dress that was ripped even more, where he could probably see my bare skin as I'd decided to forgo underwear that evening, back up to my neck where the blood remained. In one heartbeat, Matteo took a step towards me, his hands on me instantly. He lifted me into his arms, his hands squeezing my ass through the material of the dress, before he laid me back out on the countertop.

"Fuck *diavolessa*, you were bare this entire night! Are you trying to put me in an early grave?" he moaned into my ear, his tongue sliding over my bleeding neck.

I whimpered with pleasure with his mouth on me, but I craved his tongue to be in other places.

"Matteo," I whispered, my voice barely audible. I clutched at his suit jacket and drew him closer, as I tried to grind my pussy on him where he stands in between my legs.

"Filthy girl," he teased me. "You want me to play with this beautiful cunt, right here in public where anyone can walk in?"

I nodded, because I didn't think I could find the words to answer him. I was beyond turned on by the sight of him, and of my fresh kill bleeding out onto the bathroom tiles.

---

* Who Do You Want - Ex Habit

"Use your words, *dolcezza*. If I slip my fingers inside you, will I find you dripping for me?"

His fingers danced around my pussy, gliding over my entrance, but never where I wanted him to be.

"Please, Matteo," I begged, "I need you inside me."

The words had barely left my mouth before Matteo had two fingers buried knuckles deep inside me and I cried out, wanting him.

"God, I love to hear you beg, to hear you scream my name," he said, his voice hoarse.

He fucked my cunt with his hand until I was seeing stars.

"That's it, love. Take what you need, but don't you dare come. I want to taste how sweet you are on my tongue."

His words alone unraveled me. He had me hanging on by a thread, his fingers pushing me right to the edge, and as I was about to plummet over, he ripped his hand out from under my dress.

I looked down at him, my eyes burning with lust, right as he pulled my dress open to reveal my bare pussy. He used his legs to spread me open wide before him so he could see every part of me. My pussy throbbed as his eyes bore down on me, and I could feel my whole body shaking as I watched him lick his bottom lip as if I were a feast he was about to dig into.

He lifted my legs up, settling the heels of my feet on his shoulders as he licked more of the blood on my neck before he made his way between my legs.

"You're glistening baby. Fuck, I can't wait to taste you."

And then he devoured.

His tongue licked me from bottom to top, and my body was on fire. He sucked at my clit, and I shamelessly ground back into his face, longing for that friction. I was high off of him, and nothing had ever felt this good. The men before, Matteo immediately put to shame, and he hadn't even fucked me yet. I was about to crash and burn, and he must have sensed that I was close, because just as he bit down hard on my clit, he slipped a finger inside me again and hit my G-spot. I was absolutely feral. I came hard, my whole body falling back into the mirror, my breasts on the verge of spilling out of my dress.

"*Dolcezza*, you taste even better than I imagined."

His lips glistened with my juices, and he reached out, his hand grasping me by the back of the neck as he kissed me so I could taste myself on him.

"Don't you dare clean up, Emilia. I want you wet and dripping for me later when I ravish that fucking cunt," he ordered.*

My whole body failed me as I attempted to stand up, and he held me steady. He knelt before me, as I used his body to put my heels back on. And as I stood up, the top of my head coming level with his chin, he slipped out of his suit jacket and threw it over my body, the jacket falling over the giant slit in my dress.

"I'll have one of your men stay and clean up this mess. Let's get you home."

I could only nod, because I was not sure what words would come out of my mouth at that point. I was too far gone to decipher what had just transpired between us. It had been over a month of sexual frustration on both sides. Even though he'd satisfied me, I still ached for more. No man had ever gotten me off by tongue and fingers alone, only sex, and most of the time, I had to be on top. But this man had sent me on a downward spiral, and all I could think about was the next time my bodyguard would be between my legs again. Fuck the line, it had already been crossed.

---

* Stop playing Who Do You Want - Ex Habit

Matteo and I retreated quickly through the back door of the venue, where thankfully no one from the party had seen me drenched in blood and worse for wear. Dante was well-informed of the attack that had transpired, and he was fuming that Camila, *La Corredora* was able to get that close to me again. He left two men behind to take care of the assassin's body, while he left me in the capable hands of Matteo. Dante himself ventured back to the house ahead of us to check to see if there were any more threats.

Matteo opened up the door to his car and helped lower me inside, a deviant smile gracing his handsome face. He slipped inside beside me and revved the engine, his eyes falling on me.

*"The thought of you bare on my leather seats has me hard, *diavolessa.*"

His words enticed me, and I could feel myself leaving a mess on his seats. I couldn't help but tease him more after his confession.

"Are you now?" I asked, hiking my dress up further, baring myself completely to him. I brought my heel to rest on the top of his dashboard to give me the angle I so desperately needed. My fingers danced lightly over my exposed sex, and I watched as his eyes drifted over to where I played with my clit.

"Fuck, baby, that's not fair," he groaned, one hand stroking his cock through his suit.

---

* Body Language - WE ARE FURY

"Take it out, I want to see you," I declared, feeling bold.

"As you wish," he agreed, unzipping his pants and gripping his full length in his hand.

My fingers moved faster as I watched in absolute rapture at the length of his cock, his foot on the pedal pressing closer to the floor as he weaved in between traffic, desperate to get us back home. I laughed at his ferocity as he continued to steal glances at my dripping pussy. We got lost in our own ecstasy as he pulled the car directly in front of my compound, right as we both succumbed to desire.

"Now, *diavolessa*, clean up this mess," Matteo demanded, his eyes dropping down to his cock coated in his come.

My eyes widened at the sexual act he requested of me, and surprisingly I wanted nothing more to please him, to return the favor. To make him weak at the touch of my mouth this time. I wanted to show him I was in control. I twisted in my seat, not caring that my men could probably see me from the house. I leaned over the middle console and right before I swallowed his length whole, I made sure I locked eyes with him. I glided my tongue up his length, slowly and tortuously, making sure I left nothing behind.

"That's it baby, I knew you could take me," he groaned into the darkness of the car. His hands wrapped around my ponytail, pulling it tight as I sucked him off. He's large and I could feel his cock stretching my mouth wide as his length hit the back of my throat. I had never felt this turned on with a man before. Don't get me wrong, I loved giving head to a man, watching them fall helplessly to their feet as I made them see stars. It was an invigorating feeling. And Matteo's constant *fucks* every time I took him deep just made me even more wet. I felt a sharp pain on my ass cheek as he slapped it and then smoothed it over with his palm. He lifted my dress even higher, exposing my ass to the crisp air. Goosebumps covered my skin and I was not sure if it was because of the temperature or the hand that slowly drifted lower, making circles around a different hole. He applied pressure with his thumb and his other fingers slipped smoothly back to my front where they played with my clit.

"That's a good girl."

His grip on my hair tightened as I sucked him off, cleaning up the mess he had made earlier. I choked on his cock one last time, right before I felt him release again, the fast burst of hot liquid pouring down the back of my throat. I could feel his sharp, shallow breaths as I swallowed every last drop, his cussing filling the silence. After I leaned back, licking my lips for any remnants, I glanced over at him, where I found a wicked smile upon his face.

"You may just be the death of me, *diavolessa*."

CHAPTER THIRTEEN

MATTEO

I WAS BEGINNING TO BELIEVE THAT EMILIA DELUCA WAS THE actual devil in the body of a siren. She had this magnetic hold on me that I couldn't even begin to fathom to understand. I was a professional killer, the best of the best, yet she was getting the best of me. She was a labyrinth of secrets and hidden desires, and I wanted to break her apart piece by piece and unravel the mystery that was Emilia. I wanted to know everything.

Not just her secrets and desires, but *her*. I wanted to know her likes and dislikes, her fears, her favorite childhood memory, her thoughts on being a mafia queen. It was these inner thoughts that had me spiraling for an ounce of control. But, I was no longer in control anymore;, she was. She had started to wrap me around that delicate finger of hers, and I was her willing victim. I was in uncharted waters and I was struggling to stay above the surface.

I dare anyone to stare into those captivating eyes of hers and not drown in them as I was. That was just what she did. Just like the serpent wrapped around that delicious body of hers, she was beautiful, yet deadly. And I needed to remind myself of that.

I had a bad feeling leaving her alone when she excused herself to use the ladies' room. Something felt off, and I was glad I had decided to follow her, because from across the crowded room I had seen the man slip in after her. My heart had dropped into my stomach. I hadn't been sure I would be able to reach her in time. And that was the devil itself. *Time.* Not enough of it, and the never-ending battle of fighting against it.

I found her standing by the sink looking like a beautiful mess, even after she had been brutally attacked. She was missing a shoe and leaning on the counter for balance. I had scanned her body for any injuries, but deep down, I knew I was drinking in my fill of the beautiful damsel before me. Her dress was ripped, giving me a more accessible view of what lay underneath, and her breasts were practically spilling out of her dress, but it was the blood dripping down her throat that had me on edge. Her blood had spilled, and I was hard as a rock in my suit. The next thing I knew, a growl had escaped my throat and I was upon her, my hands feasting on her body, and she was letting me.

I felt her attraction to me, the lust that filled her eyes with every encounter we'd had. The missed moments between us. The blood was the match, and I had ignited it and I would let it burn until I got what I wanted. And what I wanted was her. I was definitely not disappointed, because the taste of her was euphoric. I wasn't lying to her when I told her she tasted sweet. Heavenly, if I had to put a word to her flavor, and I wasn't just talking about her lips, no, her cunt was out of this world. Her mouth had sent me over the edge of oblivion, and I was still falling.

I shook my head, clearing the image of her and what had just transpired, before I opened the car door and led her inside, where surprisingly we didn't run into Dante or anyone else, but I could hear Dante further down the hallway speaking with her guards about upping security.

We ascended her staircase, her footsteps light with the heels in her hand. Just as I was about to invite her into my room for the night to finish what we had started, she grabbed my suit jacket and silently handed it back over to me.

"Thanks for the assistance in getting me off tonight." She laughed playfully into the crook of my neck. "But I'm going to crash early tonight."

My eyes widened at the sudden dismissal, but I didn't dare push her further. I simply nodded and watched her walk into her room and close the door before I retreated back into my room across the hall. I laid in bed for hours, fantasizing about Emilia back in my car. How I'd wanted to grab her and impale her on my cock and take her right there and then, screw propriety. I wanted to own her, ravish her until she was screaming, drawing blood. I fisted my cock, replaying the images of her sprawled out before me bare on the bathroom counter. My little vixen was a filthy girl who craved not only attention, but the adrenaline rush and, oh, how I planned to give that to her. I wanted more time to explore her, to make her bend and break the way I wanted to, see what else she craved. My hand only gave me half the satisfaction that her mouth did, and I was fiending for more of her.

I tucked myself back into my joggers, still hard as a rock, and was just about to open the door to my bedroom, when I heard hers open across the hall and the soft fall of her foot-steps in the hallway heading away from my room. I slowly opened my door and caught her slipping around the corner dressed in all black and a hood.

Interesting.

Where was she going dressed like that? It was just after one in the morning. If she was going to her gym, she would've gone the other way down the hall. I ran back into my room, grabbed my shoes, and headed out after her. Everyone was asleep, besides her guards who circled the house, but it seemed she knew how to evade them, as if she had done this before.

Or maybe they know she sneaks off in the middle of the night?

I watched her enter a room, and I waited a few minutes before following her. The room was still dark, but I saw that the window was left wide open. I crossed the room in two big steps and glanced outside to find her slinking through the shadows toward a street bike. Wait, that couldn't be right. I stared out after her, my mind reeling. *Emilia rode a street bike?* How did I not know this information?

I made my way down the vines she had used, hoping that they would hold my weight as I followed the same path she had taken a minute ago. I slid into my seat and started my car. The purr of the engine reminded me of the last time I was in the seat and where Emilia's lips had been. She had almost given me a heart attack when she pulled her dress up to reveal her bare pussy, her come still glistening on those lips. This was a whole new level of torture, and she was the executioner. It had taken every ounce of willpower to keep my attention on the road and not her fingers as she played with herself on my leather seats. I was beyond tempted to crash my car, so I could replace her fingers with mine.

I only got a small taste of what she had to offer, and I was already craving my next fix. When I had made her clean me up, her pupils had dilated. We had been sitting in her driveway where any of her guards could have looked out the window and had seen her exposed in that position, but she didn't care. My girl liked the thought of someone catching her in a sexual act, and I had every intention of pushing those boundaries with her in due time.

I kept myself at a safe distance so she couldn't see my car, all the while trying to keep myself from getting distracted by the memories in this car, because if I looked real close at the passenger side, I could still see where she had dripped all over the seat. And I wasn't above pulling this car over to the side of the street and licking up her mess.

I followed her for another quarter of a mile when I saw

her pull into what looked like an abandoned factory. When she pulled around the side of the building, I followed suit but parked closer to the shadows under cover of trees and watched her slip inside a side entrance. It wasn't long before I saw a few other cars pull into the parking lot. They seemed like your average passersby. Some were already intoxicated as they met up with friends. There was an exchange of money between them, and loud, obnoxious laughs as they all poured into the front entrance where a guard was standing outside.

I followed after the group of guys and paid the guard $50 to gain entrance into the old factory. And my suspicions were correct, it was an abandoned building, however, parts of it had been set up for entertaining. There were beaten-up leather couches off to the side where some guys were sitting, knocking back shots or crouched forward doing a line of coke off some girl's ass cheeks who was splayed out on the table before them.

What was Emilia doing in a place like this?

My feet followed the sounds of shouting to a different room where I found myself overlooking a basement of sorts, where a giant cage sat in the middle of the room. Hoards of men surrounded it, some banging their fists, rattling the cage from both levels. As I got closer, I could see the old bloodstains inside the fighting ring. I glanced up to the other side to find that there was a pathway leading to the cage, cement barriers you'd see on the highways blocking drunk patrons getting to the fighters.

She was around here somewhere, but this room was completely dominated by men. I scanned the basement, where two men were fighting inside.

One was dark-skinned and had blood leaking from his nose. He was built like a machine and stood an inch taller than his opponent, who was his opposite. He was pale and bald but stocky, and he was sweating so much he was glistening under the bright lights. He ducked and weaved around his opponent, blocking every attack that came his way. But,

73

due to the height difference, the only way for the shorter opponent to get a hit in was to get close to his enemy.

I maneuvered through the crowd, trying to find Emilia hidden in this mass of heathens, when I heard a loud shout coming from the ring. I turned my head to find that the taller, dark-skinned fighter had knocked out his opponent. The crowd went wild. It was clear that this was an illegal fighting ring, and that this man himself was a favorite amongst them. I didn't pay attention to the commentator who had entered the ring to voice the winner of the fight. I could see in my peripheral vision that two burly men had stepped in to drag the unconscious man from the ring. The winning fighter had circled the cage, both fists raised in the air as he celebrated, beating on his chest. I kept my eyes low as I circled the outer perimeter of the cage, making my way down the stairs towards the cement barriers.

It wasn't until I was halfway down the stairs, when the commentator had called out the next fighter to the pit, that I heard the catcalling and whistles. I squeezed my eyes shut, dreading the worst. And when I opened my eyes, I was proven horrifically correct.

Walking into the fighting ring was Emilia.*

She wore a black mask that covered the bottom half of her face, but those blue eyes of hers glistened in the dim lighting of the basement. Her hair was up in a ponytail and it swung behind her in tandem with her steps. She was dressed in all black, in those tight athletic shorts of hers that I loved on her that showed off every toned muscle in her legs and a matching sports bra.

My heart was racing, and I clutched my chest as if I was having a heart attack, about to drop dead right here on these grimy stairs. She walked out, ignoring the crowd's taunts and sexual innuendos, and headed straight inside the ring.

---

* Lion - Saint Mesa

My eyes were blown wide in shock at the fact that she was going to fight this beast of a man. This predator. And all for sport. I tried to get closer to the cage, but the men had crowded the area, trying to ogle her as much as they could. This was wrong. Sickening.

Why is she doing this?

Emilia had entered the ring and took off her face covering, and when her eyes looked up at her opponent, she graced him with one of her seductive taunts. She was goading him, just like she had Tobias. She was playing with fire, and I was scared that she was going to get burned. I couldn't protect her from here.

Where are her guards? They can't possibly know about this?

My senses left me as I threw myself at the fence, trying to gain her attention, but she was zoned out. My fists hammered on the wire fence, but the sound was drowned out by the intoxicated men surrounding me, mimicking my movements. She didn't even notice me or the crowd before her. Her face was a mask of stone. All mischief left her eyes and what replaced it had my skin crawling and the hairs on my arms raised. Before me, I saw the *Serpent Queen*. The look that fell upon her face was one of death and destruction. She wasn't going to hold back. There was no mercy written there, not in those eyes. I peered closer at her then, and the blue eyes I would've happily drowned in had been replaced with a dark indigo hue, a shade shy of being midnight black. It was like she had switched off her senses, as if a new person had control of her, possessing her thoughts.

The bell sounded, the echo ringing in my ear, a cruel reminder that the fight had been initiated. There was no turning back now. Emilia and her opponent circled one another around the small ring like the predators they were. She didn't smile at him anymore. She was tight-lipped and stone cold, while he jeered at her with sexual snippets and the crowd furthered his agenda with their own taunts. She ignored it all, nothing reflecting on her face to show that she was bothered at all by what they said.

The fighter swung a right hook towards her face, and she ducked under his arm, inching closer, jabbing him hard in his ribs, before dancing away from him. But she wasn't quick enough, as he swung at her, wrapping his hand around her hair and pulled her back into him, where his fist met her nose. The hit had stunned her, her eyes widening at the impact. Her eyes focused back in on him, as he lifted her body and threw her hard at the wire cage. She hit the floor with a sickening thud and I stopped breathing. My own fists curled tightly, my nails creating half moon craters in the palms of my hand. I felt blood pool in the crevices as my eyes locked in on her opponent. Death awaited him.

She stood up, spitting blood from her mouth, and then her lips turned into a sneer. She raised her hands once more, readying herself for his next attack. He charged at her, pinning her up against the cage, his hands reached out toward her as if to choke her. His hands wrapped around her, but she had raised her arms and brought her elbows down hard to his inner arms, making them drop. I watched as she then leaned forward, head-butting him. He soared backward through the cage, his hands clutching at his face. When he pulled them away, blood poured from his broken nose. From where I stood, I could hear him uttering curse words at her.

Atta girl.

She didn't wait for him to get his bearings; she went on the offensive and came flying at him with an assortment of punches and kicks. Some hit their mark, but her last kick he caught in midair and he used her momentum to bring her to the ground. The sickening crack of her knee hitting the concrete sent a jolt through my entire body. She bit her lip, biting back the pain. She didn't even have time to fully feel the impact before the fighter was driving his knee into her face. The force knocked her head back as blood flew from her mouth. My hands came out in front of me to grip the fence, willing it to bend to my command. I needed to get to her, but I couldn't.

The fighter grew cocky as he circled the floor of the cage, riling up the crowd and the cheers that echoed back were repulsive to my ears as I desperately tried to will her eyes to look at me. But, she just wiped the blood from her mouth, stood up and launched herself high in the air at her opponent, doing the exact same move she had done to me. She won herself some shouts of glory from the crowd with the take-down. Emilia wrapped her legs around his neck as they grappled on the cement floor. With her knee gruesome and bruised, I could tell she was trying to get a good grip in her headlock but was slipping, and her opponent knew it too as he aimed fists at her injured knee. After a few hits, she lost her grip on the headlock and he used that to his advantage as he flipped his body around so that he was on top of her. But her legs were still holding tightly around him. She hadn't completely given up. There was still hope. He lifted himself into the air, ready to bring her down hard back to the cement for the win, when her hands grabbed the top of the fighting cage, and she used her momentum to get a better hold on him as her legs began to choke him out once more.

The crowd watched on at the pure entertainment before them, shouts in her favor, chants in his, but she was winning as I watched the muscle in her legs constrict and flex as they crushed his windpipe. I peeked a glance at the opponent and I watched with glee as his eyes rolled to the back of his head and his body went limp. As he fell to the ground, Emilia released her hands and launched herself, landing in a crouch on the floor next to his unconscious body. She tried to land as softly as she could with her injury, but the impact of her jump made her take a step forward, favoring her bad leg. She looked around at the crowd, her stone cold face back on display like a mask. She didn't wait for the commentator to call her name as the winner. She turned her back to him and started to head back toward the locker room. I followed her movements as I ran after her, my sanity falling somewhere behind me on the metal staircase as I raced after the women I thought I was falling for.

CHAPTER FOURTEEN

EMILIA

*I MADE MY WAY THROUGH THE CHANTING CROWD, NOT CARING about the glory of winning the fight. I didn't fight in these illegal fighting rings for respect or attention. I fought because I needed to feel something. The beauty of pain is that it forces you to stay in the moment, to feel everything at once. Bruises healed, but scars left a mark, even the ones that weren't always visible. But sometimes I felt like I deserved the pain that came my way. I was a sinner that was hellbound, there was no doubt about that. I had heard about this place in passing at one of Grant's events. I came here maybe twice a month when I desperately needed to feel something. I had learned that feeling anything was better than feeling nothing at all.

I had been in that dark place a long time ago. Where the demons came out to play, but they weren't always polite. They didn't wait for the cover of night; no, they liked to circle their prey in the light too, and I always came out as the victim. For too long, I had suffered in silence. No one cared about my screams, and when I realized no one was coming to save me, I'd stopped screaming completely.

---

* Power is Power (feat. the Weeknd & Travis Scott - SZA

I had gone numb. I hadn't wanted to feel the things that were happening to me. The slow torturous strain it was putting on my psyche. I was a prisoner, sold into a profitable business, with no escape in sight. The only way you escaped that kind of prison was in a body bag. And when I had realized no one was coming to save me, I had accepted death as my savior.

Inside the locker room, I stared at the damage in the mirror. My lip had been split open and I could still taste the blood dripping from my nose. There was also a massive bruise forming underneath my eye and I had injured my ribs again in the fight, but my knee was my main concern. I would definitely need to have my doctor take a look at it.

No one knew what I did on these nights, not even Dante. I was a good fighter and, for the most part, I tried to keep any injuries to parts of my body I could easily cover up. But the black eye I'd be sporting by this morning would be harder to disguise without heavy makeup. I knew I'd never get caught fighting in these rings, not when Grant ran them.

The fluorescent lights were unforgiving as I scanned my face one last time before turning from the mirror. Most fighters would feel a euphoric high from winning a fight, but all I felt was nothing. No high, no glory ... just an aching hollowness, my mind still numb and void. The only time I felt something was inside that ring. As I'd looked over myself in the mirror, I'd realized it had been at least two months since I last fought. Over the last month so much had consumed my mind. From losing three of my men, to *La Corredora* encroaching onto my territory, to the secret society's offer that still plagued my every thought, and now to Matteo. When I thought more about why I hadn't been at the fighting ring in a while, it all trickled back to Matteo. I came to fight so I could feel something, even if temporarily, but these last two months my interactions with Matteo, no matter how small, had been substantial enough to the point where I didn't need to blow off steam like usual. Tonight was the exception. Tonight I'd felt too much with Matteo, and I'd panicked.

My mind was so chaotic, I just needed an outlet to shut out the voices. Fighting helped with that, even if it was only a temporary reprieve.

I was the only woman that fought in these fights, so I didn't have to worry about anyone coming into the locker room after me. I stripped down and changed into black leather pants and a matching jacket before lacing up my boots. The temperature had most likely dropped since I had been here, and I wasn't going to go back home in those winds in just a sports bra and shorts.

I made my way through the dark, dank hallway leading to the alleyway outside the old factory, the crisp autumn air hitting me in the face like an assault worse than what I had suffered in the ring. My leather jacket did nothing to block out the onslaught of Chicago weather bearing down on my exposed skin. I felt the goosebumps on my skin rise from the chill, but the hair on the back of my neck started to stand on edge and I knew it wasn't because of the drop in temperature. I was being watched.

I scanned my surroundings, finding no one around. I chalked it up to everything that had happened over the course of the month, but my gut was telling me otherwise. Slowly and quietly, I pulled the gun from my bag and inched closer to the opening of the alley, this time on high alert.

I heard a crash in the distance, a broken bottle hitting pavement as voices drifted to my ears. I watched as four drunk guys left the fight, their raucous laughter echoing down the alley, snippets of their conversation about the dark beauty sweeping the floor with Maddox.

They didn't see me lurking in the shadows, watching their every move. I waited until I could no longer hear their voices and I felt myself relax. I walked slowly backward towards my bike, but right as I lowered my gun to my side, I felt hot, heavy breathing run down my neck and my muscles tensed as I mentally prepared myself for a fight.*

"You are just full of surprises, little minx," Matteo purred into my ear. I couldn't stop the shiver in my body from his heated words, but I prayed that he chalked it up to the autumn air.

"You followed me!" I seethed at him. This fighting ring was one of the few outlets I had in this world. This was where I blew off steam without my guards hovering down my neck. It was my chance to just be a woman on the verge of a plummeting cliff, an abyss of darkness waiting for me below. If I was just some woman fighting in the ring, most people would chalk it up to "issues" or "on the verge of a mental breakdown" and don't get me wrong, I was straddling the line of both, but I wasn't just some woman. I was the mafia Donna of the DeLuca clan here in Chicago. I would never be normal. This was sacred territory to me, and Matteo was invading.

"If you didn't want to be followed, then you shouldn't have made it so easy to find you, *diavolessa*. If I was able to follow you so easily, so can your enemy."

A part of me knew he was speaking the truth, though I wouldn't dare admit he was right. I had dropped my guard, and he knew it.

Leaving my home without a guard was reckless and stupid, but I just didn't care. I would never admit to him that he was right, so instead I resorted to anger and irritation and turned around to slap him with the butt of my gun. Only, he saw the attack coming and grabbed my wrist before the weapon could strike his face. He held my wrist in the palm of his hand, his grip firm.

"You're slipping, Emilia," he taunted, putting pressure on a point in my wrist. My hand jackknifed open involuntarily when he did, my gun falling from my grasp. He caught it in

---

* Stop playing Power is Power (feat. The Weeknd & Travis Scott) - SZA

his other hand, not once letting go of mine. With my gun in the palm of his hand, he used the barrel of the gun to stroke over my breasts.

"Guess I just got lucky it was you that found me in this alleyway and not *La Corredora.*"

He continued to swirl the tip of my gun over my breasts, my nipples traitorous bitches as they hardened under his watchful gaze. His smug smile graced his face as they peaked through the thin material. He glided the tip further down my body, backing me up ever so slowly until the backs of my thighs hit my bike.

"Are you sure about that, *diavolessa*?"

He edged me down onto the seat of my bike, his hand sneaking around my body to lift my legs to rest on his hips. The only thing keeping my body upright and balanced was the hold he still had on my wrist. If he let go, I would fall. And there were many reasons why I didn't want him to let go, many reasons I didn't want to dive into.

"I never said I would show you mercy," he whispered in my ear. *I bucked under the weight of his words and what he was implying. He moved in closer to my body, closing the gap between us.

He moved my gun lower still, until I could feel the muzzle pressed firmly on my sex. I questioned my morals at that moment, and was thoroughly convinced that I needed therapy, because everything Matteo was doing and whispering to me had me soaked.

"And why wouldn't you show me mercy?" I panted, my pussy grinding along the barrel of my gun, aching for more friction, my mind silently begging him to do something more sinful to me.

"I couldn't stand the thought of that man making you bleed," he stated, his movements coming more rapidly as he

---

* Worship - Ari Abdul

rubbed my hot center. "If you are going to bleed, it's going to be by my teeth, just so I can lick it off of you."

His strokes came more viciously then.

"The sight of you on your knees before him," he seethed, stilling his hand movements before nibbling at my earlobe. Quietly, he whispered to me, "Had me seeing red. Only time you should be on your knees is if you have my cock stretching your throat."

He placed my hands on the back of his neck, drawing him closer to my body. He moved the gun upward then, the muzzle sweeping across my breasts once more, only to glide over my pouty lips as he spoke again.

"And the bruises marked on your skin, I can't stand the sight of them. If anyone is going to be leaving you with bruises, it'll be by my hand as I choke you while you come on this cock," he declared, making a statement as his free hand came up to grasp my throat, the muzzle of the gun dipping low between my breasts.

"You put me through the ringer tonight, *diavolessa*. And we never finished what we started, so now, I am going to make you suffer tenfold."

He tucked my gun into the waistline of his jeans, right as his mouth came down on my neck, biting hard. The punctures of his teeth breaking my skin made me arch my back, my grip on the back of his neck death-like as I held on through the hot, searing pain that lit me up from the inside. His hands dipped into my tank top and he pulled my breasts free and began lightly stroking my tightened nipples. I rocked my hips forward into his hardening cock, relishing in the heated friction between us. Despite the frigid air, my body felt like I was burning in flames. And suddenly, I wanted no barriers between us at all. I wanted his skin on mine, fuck the fact that it was forty-two degrees and we were in public.

"Matteo," I cried out, using my legs around his hips to get a better angle.

He stopped sucking at my neck, only to continue to lick and kiss down my chest to my perky nipples. They were only too eager to meet his hot breath as he took them into his mouth. He was all too generous, taking his time licking, biting and sucking on my nipples.

To be frank, I was so turned on by this man that the inside of my pants felt like a slip and slide. No fingers, no tongue, and certainly no cock had entered me, and this man had brought me on the precipice of an orgasm.

I honestly questioned who the fuck he was and why no man was ever able to make me this wild and free.

He bit down hard on my nipple, and I bucked wildly, an onslaught of curse words leaving my mouth.

"Fuck!" I screamed.

He worked fast, his hands making quick work of the button on my pants, before lifting and sliding the leather material down my hips, past my thighs, and finally down to my ankles. He leaned down his face in between my open legs and inhaled deeply. Without warning, he plunged his tongue in between my wet folds and licked me from bottom to top, hovering right at my clit. His tongue had me in a frenzy and I pushed back into him, clutching his hair to push him deeper inside me.

"Fuck, yes," I moaned into the dark.

I caught glimpses of his outline in the bare moonlight. His untamed onyx curls, his broad shoulders as he worked at my pussy.

"Oh my god!" I shouted, as I felt my legs tighten and constrict, an entire body tremor coursing through me. My orgasm hit me —blinding and euphoric—and before I could even come down from the high, Matteo had already thrusted his cock fully inside me, buried to the hilt.

CHAPTER FIFTEEN

MATTEO

BEING INSIDE OF EMILIA WAS EXHILARATING. I HADN'T BEEN lying when I said she had put me through the ringer. Watching her fight in that ring tonight, the floor splattered with her blood and bruises marring her skin, had me seeing red. It took every ounce of will power in me not to leave her out here and stroll right back into that club, locate the fighter named Maddox, and end his life for even daring to raise a finger toward her. But the subtle, playful smile on Emilia's face held me captive.

Her lips parted, and her breath hitched when I dragged the tip of her gun down over her peaked nipples and further along her body. The confident tilt of her head gave me the push to drive her backward onto the seat of her bike. I wanted to ruin her, right here in this alley tonight. Hearing her scream my name in ecstasy again was heaven in its purest form.

I wanted to push her to her absolute limits, drive her insane as much as she did to me. I kissed and sucked and traced my tongue along the outline of the snake winding its way around her slender neck before trailing my kisses further down to her supple and eager breasts. Her tawny nipples were straining against her fitted tank, begging to be touched. I ripped her breasts free from their confines and took each soft nipple into my mouth. The taste of her was sensational, amber musk and her sweat hit my tongue like a tsunami. My cock hardened under her touch.

When I bit down hard on her nipple, she let out an onslaught of curse words, and hearing Emilia draw out the word *fuck* sent all the blood rushing to my aching cock. All semblance of control and intentions I had to take this torturously slow for her evaporated with that one word. I scrambled to unbutton her pants and drag them down the length of her curvy body. When the material fell around her ankles, I took in the glorious sight before me.

Emilia was perched on the edge of her Ducati Streetfighter, legs spread wide, her pussy glistening under the moonlight, and I swear the sight before me would have put Van Gogh to shame. She was a masterpiece and no artist or God could paint her to perfection. I just knew deep down they wouldn't get her colors right. Like how her inky black hair fell down in waves, woven in starlight, or how her eyes were a piercing deep turquoise that held an intensity of a million burning suns. They wouldn't be able to capture her full, soft lips that could swallow me whole. She was ethereal in the light of the full moon, and I was her favored casualty. I drank in the sight of her. Emilia in her rawest form, unguarded and in her element, was like staring at Medusa. She was beautiful but such beauty was finite. And with a beauty like Emilia's, you could get lost in her radiance, held prisoner like a statue.

But if I were to lose my sight, if this was the last vision I had, well, she would be worth it.

I sank to my knees on the cold, hard ground and drank in the sight of her. I inhaled her aroma, letting the power of her overwhelm my senses, suffocating me in all her glory. My tongue darted out to taste her once more, and when that sweet, tangy flavor of Emilia coated my tongue, it was like an epiphany ignited in my veins. Here I was on my knees for this woman, a woman I had studied for weeks, but not truly knowing her until now. I did not get on my knees for anyone. I've tasted good pussy before, I wasn't some gangly teenager just discovering what a vagina was and all the ways you can make a girl come. But in this very moment, I was on my knees for this woman, worshiping the ground she walked on, because right there, Emilia DeLuca became my religion.

*I licked and sucked her, letting this adrenaline rush fill my body, because her taste was like a drug. She was addictive, and I knew I could never stop. I lapped her up like a starved man, drowning in the abyss of her. And I did what I do best, I made her suffer tenfold, as promised. I tortured and teased her orgasm right out of her, until she was begging for my cock.

"Come for me, my filthy girl. I want you to come all over this sweet bike of yours. That way you can think of how wet I make you every time you ride it."

Her long nails sank into my skin, pulling me closer to where she wanted me. I relented, and she wasted no time using her hands to spring my cock free from my pants. Pre-come dripped from the head of my cock, and I watched as her eyes hungrily followed its path. Her finger reached out to catch it, and I greedily stared at her as she took her finger into her mouth and sucked. Her cheeks hollowed out as she sucked on her finger like a lollipop. She released it, her mouth making a *pop* sound as she did, and I pounced.

I couldn't wait one second longer. I needed to be with this woman. I wanted to be buried inside her tight cunt and I was done denying myself that feeling. Emilia licked her lips as she took in the sight of me. She gave me a ravenous look as I sank myself inside her, her eyes rolling to the back of her head as her body adjusted to my size. She squirmed at the edge of the bike in anticipation of my next thrust, and I smiled coyly down at her, basking in her impatience.

---

* Toxic - 2WEI

She was going to ruin me, there was no doubt in my mind about that, but I sure as hell was going to make sure I destroyed her in the process. I slowly pulled out of her, a sad sigh in the middle of my chest at the loss of her warmth. I didn't give her time to readjust as I plunged back inside her, a gasp escaping her as I took what I wanted from her. Over and over again, I drove myself deep inside Emilia, watching her as she wore her emotions all over her face for me to read and dissect. Her mouth hung open in a constant "O" shape, her breaths short and shallow, in perfect sync with my thrusts, and if I had to guess, I would say her nails had pierced my skin in her frenzy.

"That's it. You're taking my cock like such a good girl."

I felt her pussy tighten around my cock at my words, and I almost blew my load right then and there. She was sucking the life right out of me, and all I could do to keep from going under was to tighten my hold on her.

Around us I could hear the revelers in the distance shouting and laughing as they continued on with their night, and I prayed that they'd avoid this alley. I'd gut anyone on sight if they saw Emilia displayed bare like this for anyone to see. Her body was for me to admire, to worship; only me.

I felt the November night reach out and clutch us in its claws; the temperature had dropped significantly since we'd been outside and I could see the slight goosebumps coasting along Emilia's exposed skin. I continued my ruination of her, taking in the glorious sight before me.

Her long, luscious mane was tied back in a ponytail and I grabbed a fistful of it in my hands and yanked. She bit down on her lip, but otherwise embraced the pain. Her pale blue eyes shined like a beacon in the night, a flame dancing within. Her lips were puffy and red from the cold air, and I wanted to sink my teeth into them.

My eyes trailed lower to the head of the snake branded into her skin, eyeing me like prey. Its beady eyes reflected in the moonlight, almost making me think that it was alive under her olive-colored skin. I dragged my gaze further, to where they rested on her bouncing tits. Her nipples were fully peaked and red as cherries. I watched them go up and down in a circle and I leaned forward, taking one into my mouth. I swirled my tongue back and forth, my teeth scraping along her bud as she cried out in bliss, her tight cunt squeezing me once more. I switched to her other breast and gave it the same treatment, while my hand slipped between our bodies. Pressing firmly down on her clit, I began to roll my thumb in a circular motion, gazing at Emilia's expression the entire time as she slowly shattered into pieces around me.

She was on the precipice of her orgasm and I drank in every last detail to re-play back later when I was alone. Her head was thrown back, her elongated neck stretching as much as it could go with my hand still pulling viciously on her hair. I didn't ease up, nor would I. Despite the cooler temperature, I watched as a bead of sweat dripped down the slope of her neck and disappeared between her breasts. I bent her back more on her bike, her nails digging in deeper as she held on tight. I met it right as it crested the curve, tracing my tongue up the path it had taken. She inhaled deeply at my action, and I smiled.

All that time, my thumb never let up, the speed of it changing course, constantly driving her wild. I stared down at our bodies melding together like she was my missing puzzle piece. I couldn't describe this feeling, other than to say it felt like I was drawn to her by an invisible string. I felt her hand lift from my arm and on instinct I gripped her tightly to prevent her from falling, but when I gazed into those burning blue irises of hers, no flicker of terror was there. As she peered into my green eyes I swear I heard her opal eyes whisper back, *"I trust you."*

Her hand rested gracefully on my cheek, and our intense eye contact never wavered as I continued to drive into her.

And when she tightened one last time, squeezing my cock to the brink of suffocation, I felt the flame ignite within her body at her orgasm and the color of her eyes slightly darkened to that of the Tyrrhenian sea. She didn't look away from me as she rode out her orgasm on my cock, and it wasn't long after that I slowly followed her right off that cliff. She pulled me in deep as I came inside her and kissed her. I felt my come drip down onto her leather seat and I smiled at the thought of us leaving our mark on her bike. A memory for her to relive every time she sank that gorgeous ass of hers onto this seat.*

"I fight to remind myself that I am alive," she confessed to me in between entwined breaths, her forehead resting on my chest. She didn't move to cover herself afterwards, her body still on full display.

After everything that had just transpired between us, her divulging that truth of hers to me was the furthest from my mind.

---

* Stop playing Toxic - 2WEI

CHAPTER SIXTEEN

EMILIA

I PULLED BACK FROM MATTEO, ONLY JUST REALIZING I WAS still naked in front of him. Not one to shy away from nudity, I stood there with my leather pants around my ankles, my pussy raw and spent from the size of him and my breasts spilling over my tank top. If there was one thing I'd learned about Matteo tonight, it's that he was a man of his word.

I was a powerful woman in this city, and yet my bodyguard had me begging and pleading to be fucked. Not only that, but I'd found myself surprisingly at his mercy, exposing the truths of my past. I dropped low to gather my pants in my hand and shimmied back into them, the movement jostling my still exposed breasts. Out of the corner of my eye, I saw his cock twitch in his hands as he made to tuck himself back into his pants.

His hand rose to cradle my face in his palm, and I leaned into his touch, savoring this candid moment between us. The silence felt detrimental, as if one sound would destroy this sincere moment between us. I closed my eyes, basking in these last moments of peace. I felt the faint whisper of the wind at the loss of his hand on my face, but I didn't dare open my eyes. Because I knew once I did, I'd have to face reality once more, and I didn't want to go back, not yet anyway. His hand grabbed hold of my jaw and tilted my face up.

*"Open your eyes, *il mio diavolessa*."

I debated keeping my eyes closed in protest, but his grip was unrelenting. I slowly opened my eyes, only to be drawn into his forest-colored eyes that I thought I might actually get lost in.

"If you need a reminder that you're alive, let me be the one to show you."

I searched his eyes, looking for something that I wouldn't find. This moment was fleeting between us, and relationships were a fickle thing in my line of work. Love was not on the table for me. It couldn't be.

"Use me, Emilia," he continued, "Use me to your heart's desire."

He stepped closer to me, his other hand dropping to my waist and pulling me in until our faces were inches apart. This right here felt more intimate than what we just did to one another only two minutes before. Despite the fact that he had exposed me to the world for anyone to see, that hadn't made me feel vulnerable, it made me feel *something*. Something that I hadn't felt in, well, I think ever.†

I get lost in my trip down memory lane to my childhood

---

* I Walk the Line - Halsey
† Stop playing Walk the Line - Halsey

days. Growing up with a father who didn't always show his emotions, I'd never experienced much of what love was supposed to be. His version was the basic staples of what could be considered love. A roof over my head, nice clothes on my body, food on the table and not a want for anything, because we had everything we needed. We had money, protection, and power growing up with the DeLuca name. It was a name that was feared by our enemies, and revered amongst those who were loyal to my family. But I desired a deeper love. My father hadn't taught me how to ride a bike, and my mother was dead, so I'd had no one to braid my hair as a little girl. Instead, my father had put a weapon in my hands and taught me how to shoot.

And his final act of love in his eyes was to marry me off to another affluent Italian family that existed in our world. He'd thought he was making us richer, stronger, and more protected, but he'd failed at all three. Seventeen, not yet an adult, and yet I was married off like I was a piece of property. The unjust life of a girl in the mafia. I had no rights. I either belonged to my father or to my husband.

When I'd first met Romeo, it wasn't hard to conclude that he was a handsome man. Hair the color of mine, brown eyes so dark they were almost black, and a body built for women to swoon over. Yes, he was a good-looking man, but regardless of his looks, my gut told me he was a snake slithering in the weeds, waiting to attack. I had made eye contact with Dante from across the foyer and read his face. He glowered at the man that stood in my family home, dressed in a black three-piece suit, hand hovering over his gun as if he was the enemy. I had no choice in the matter, in the deal that my father and Romeo had struck up, and that night I was whisked away by the Morelli family. I later learned that Romeo was ten years older than me. He'd needed a wife on his arm to come into some money and to take over his family business, and I was the shiny prize to make that dream a reality.

On my eighteenth birthday, I was married off to Romeo Morelli. Finally an adult, the Morelli family hung me up like a doll while they slapped on makeup, pulled my hair into a half up style, and put me in a wedding dress that was elegant yet stylish. It was as white as the first fallen snow, with intricate bead work that fell around me like fallen stars. It had an A-line silhouette with a slit that ran the length of my thigh, and the bodice melded to my frame, pushing my newly blossomed breasts upward.

I was a sight to behold, and if not for the occasion, I would have admired myself in the dress. In spite of my age, I knew the Morelli family had specifically chosen this dress for me to wear to make me look older than I was. They wanted the guests to forget that I was just barely legal and that this marriage wasn't something to turn a blind eye to.

Romeo and I consummated the marriage in a hotel room with eye witnesses. Not only were both our fathers and Dante there, but Romeo's creepy, younger twin brothers were also there to watch. My first time was not gentle or fun. It wasn't what they had described it to be in the romance books I read or the movies I watched as a teenager. Romeo didn't make love to me; he didn't caress my body, he didn't appease me by telling me it would be okay. No, Romeo fucked me on our wedding night, and he wasn't gentle about it either. His big hands had ripped my beautiful dress open wide so he could gain easier access to what I held near and dear to my heart. In moments, my dress was shredded fabric on the floor at my feet, and the lingerie his family had picked out were the only garments left covering my dignity.

I'd laid there on the bed like a doll, fragile and lifeless as he fucked me into womanhood. My first time was not magical or filled with love. No, it was lust that coated Romeo's eyes that night, their chocolate brown coal-like in the barely dimmed lighting, and every thrust inside me was painful as he tore me open wide. He wasn't gentle with his hands either, because when he came inside me, spent and satiated, there was nothing left but blood on the sheets, hand prints branded into my skin that even with time would never fade, and my virtue viscerally ripped from me for all those inside the room to bear witness to.

Once he'd cleaned himself up and left the room, they led my father out as well, but Dante had stayed and cared for me by shielding me with his jacket to preserve what dignity I had left. He'd known what I would be walking into and had prepped a bag of fresh clothes for me to change into. I left my own wedding early that night, alone, afraid, and in pain.

Life and sex didn't get any better for me after my marriage. He may have been my husband in name, but that was it. It wasn't sex, nor was it fucking my husband in my eyes. I didn't want to die in bed with this monster, nor did I want his cock inside me, not when he was vile in bed to me. Bruises marked my skin, but he was smart enough to leave them in places where society wouldn't find them.

He was a monster. When he got bored of raping his wife who couldn't bear him children, he got creative. Not being able to get pregnant was my saving grace at that moment. But it was also the match that lit my world on fire when he grew tired of me and resorted to other means. I wasn't strong enough tonight to get that vulnerable with Matteo. I'd been young, naive and helpless then. I wasn't any of those things now.

*"Where did you go just now?" he asked me, pulling me out of the dark place I had drifted off too.

"No place worth revisiting," I heard myself say.

"I'm serious, Emilia, let me be what brings the light back into your eyes."

My head reared back slightly at his comment, but I don't get far from him with his hand still cupping my jaw.

"What makes you think there was a light to begin with?"

He opened his mouth to answer and then paused, contemplating for a minute before finally speaking. "You are many things, Emilia DeLuca, but a liar is not one of them."

I felt chastised being caught, and not because of my blatant lie to him, but for being seen. For being heard behind bold-faced lies and pretty masks that hid buried pain. He read me like an open book and that was a dangerous line to hover near. My truth was something I kept tucked away in the deepest pits of my mind. Years of battling my will to heal were overshadowed by my mind's effort to block out memories that would devastate me once more.

"I know you felt something," he continued. "Even if it was a fraction of lust, I know you felt something awaken inside you, because I felt it too. And I am not above riding out this feeling with you, because I have now tasted you and felt your tight pussy, and I am a madman at your mercy because I crave more from you. Whatever you have to offer, I will take. I'll give you what you hunger for, what you thirst for, what you spend nights looking for in dirty fighting rings."

I studied his face, taking in every word he said to me before caving to hear his answer.

"And what is that something I am looking for?"

He released his hold on me, backing up toward his car as he called out from down the alley.

"Pleasure."

---

* Continue playing Walk the Line - Halsey

CHAPTER SEVENTEEN

MATTEO

WHILE THE HOUSE WAS ASLEEP, I WAS WIRED, NOT HAVING slept a wink last night after my encounter with Emilia in the alley. After I had retreated to my car, I blasted the heat as I waited for her to pull out on her bike, so I could make sure she got home safe and sound. Emilia may have been a badass in her own right, but she was terrifyingly reckless going out alone with no back-up. I wanted to blast Dante when I saw him next, for not knowing about her extracurriculars, though I figured it may be useless. I could already picture her face if I was to reveal her secret: permanent scowl, eyebrows raised and her snarky comment about how no one told her what she could and couldn't do.

Unless that person was me. Cocky, yes, but my job was to keep her safe. Telling Emilia what she couldn't do, specifically in the bedroom, well, I'd have to say I think that was her fore-play. She got off being told what to do. Like a *good girl*. So, yes, unless that person was me, Emilia wasn't going to listen to what anyone told her.

It had been five hours since I had returned to Emilia's estate, and I'd spent that time reminiscing about the image of her and her body on display or taking a cold shower. My mind

98

played her moans repeatedly, to the point I contemplated crossing the hall and letting myself into her bed and going for round two. I only stopped myself from doing just that because I knew she had been through a lot last night, and she needed more rest, especially since there was much more I planned to do to her later.

With sleep clearly not in the cards for me, I slipped on a red tee, black joggers, and my running shoes, prepared to sweat this built-up tension out with a ten-mile run.

Upon slipping out my bedroom door, I hovered just outside Emilia's, praying to catch her awake. As casually as I could muster, I pressed my ear to her door, waiting with bated breath, but no movement came from the other side. I sighed heavily, defeated, and made my way downstairs, swiping a banana off the dining room table. *I jogged outside to fog blanketing the ground, a noticeable chill in the air. Chicago in autumn could be quite beautiful, yet eerie. The sun had started to ascend in the distance, cutting through the morning mist and painting Emilia's estate in a golden light. Here where Emilia lived, the air still smelled fresh, and I breathed it in, appreciating it before I made my way into the city.

I nodded over to the guards by the gate, and they subtly nodded back, letting me pass. In less than a half hour, I was in the heart of the city. The feeling of the chill air grounded me as I ran through the streets. I loved running in the early mornings before the sun woke the rest of the city. It was as quiet as it would get before the white noise of conversations of strangers and the steady thrum of horns from aggravated taxi drivers. It was peaceful.

I jogged in place parallel with the Navy Pier, basking in my city for the briefest of moments. The Chicago skyline was breathtakingly beautiful from this vantage point. The skyscrapers shimmered under the sun's radiant light, casting

---

* Prisoner - Raphael Lake, Aaron Levy, Daniel Ryan Murphy

the city below in a warm hue. Beyond those skyscrapers, a tempting seductress was probably just waking up, and I found my mind wandering, thoughts of what Emilia looked like when she woke up in the morning at the forefront of my mind.

I closed my eyes to the image of Emilia sprawled out in her bed, the waves of her hair fanning out around her like a sea creature's tentacles on her pillow, a sleepy smile appearing on her face as she stretched, pushing her body deeper into the mattress. My thoughts drifted, wondering if she wore lingerie to bed, or better yet, did she sleep naked under those sheets. Was her face naked of makeup, or did she have mascara marks from falling asleep without washing her face? I couldn't stop myself from thinking these things about her, let alone imagining what it would be like to wake her up in a different way. With my face buried between her thighs, the taste of her on my tongue while her breathy moans graced my ears. I felt the erection in my pants at the idea of having Emilia as break-fast and I reached out to grasp the railing in front of me. I took a few shaky breaths in, trying to calm my breathing and pushing my traitorous thoughts far out into Lake Michigan. It was then I felt the hairs on the back of my neck rise and go still. My body stiffened, but it was too late. Four men in masks threw a bag over my head and started to drag me backwards into a waiting van. I hadn't even seen or heard the van approach, my thoughts of Emilia having distracted me.

Instinct took over, and I used whatever weapons I had at my disposal. I began throwing elbows and shifting my weight with the intention of potentially catching one of these bastards off balance. One of my elbows managed to strike one of my attackers, and I felt him loosen his grip. By the time I had freed one of my arms, I felt the impact ricochet through my body as I landed roughly in the back of the van. Before I had a chance to get to a sitting position where I could defend myself, I felt the all too familiar sound of cable ties squeezing around my wrists.

Fuck.

I mentally prepared myself for what I was going to face. When the bag lifted and my eyes focused on the people in front of me, the last person I expected to find was Tobias. Sitting directly next to my friend was **FBI SSA Richards.**[*]

"What the fuck is this?" I demanded, my eyes locked directly on Tobias, ignoring the agent all together.

His eyes didn't reach mine, ashamed of the position he was in.

"Mr. Ricci," SSA Richards started. "It was my understanding that the FBI hired you and your "thugs for hire" to complete a task. A task that included getting proof of Miss DeLuca's illegal activities, a task that the FBI paid you handsomely for, if I'm not mistaken," he droned on.

I continued to glare at my second in command, my eyes refusing to shift from him. I ignored Richards and once again spoke only to Tobias.

"Who do you work for?" I spat out at him.

Tobias wasn't just my second in command, he was my friend. He'd been part of the mission that killed five of our close friends. I knew he felt the same pain I did, blamed himself like I did. This felt like betrayal.

Tobias chanced a look at me, and regret flooded his eyes as he worked up the courage to face me.

"I work for you ..." his voice trailed off, as the pretentious bastard next to him interrupted.

"He may work for you, but you both work for the FBI, and it has been weeks since you were initiated into Emilia's crew, and yet you've been radio silent since the car bombing."

"Because there's nothing to tell," I replied, keeping my

---

[*] Stop playing Prisoner - Raphael Lake, Aaron Levy, Daniel Ryan Murphy

voice stable, even though all I wanted to do was punch this fucking dick in his face.

SSA Richards forces a polite smile, as he chuckles to himself.

"Oh, on the contraire, Matteo. There is much to tell," he said with pleasure.

That pulled me from Tobias, and as I laid my eyes on the FBI agent before me, sounds erupted from his cell phone, sounds I was very well-versed in, because those sounds were Emilia's moans of pleasure.

My blood boiled beneath my skin, but I controlled my face, careful to not reveal any emotions as this prick shoves his phone further into my face. The video footage on his phone was from an aerial vantage point, maybe the rooftop of the abandoned building, but it revealed Emilia in a compromising position. From this viewpoint, you could see the top of her tits, and her bare legs wrapped around my back, but thank fuck, not much else. He played the whole thing for me, watching me intently as I took in the scene on the phone. If I wasn't currently in the position I was in, I'd ask him for a copy of the tape, but I knew deep down the amateur footage was nothing compared to my memory of that night.

"You were supposed to be getting surveillance on her, not fucking her in alleys," he leered down at me.

My nails dug into my palms, leaving bloodied half-moon marks behind as I tried to control my tone with the man before me.

"I do what needs to get done, in whatever way necessary. That is what you hired me and my—what did you call them again?" I paused, pretending to think. "*Thugs for hire* do for our employers. In this case, the closer I get to Emilia, the faster her walls come down. And she will open up to me. With *La Corredora* breathing down her neck, Emilia is bound to break and make a mistake," I explained to him,, "And when she does I will be there."

He leaned back in his seat, contemplating the half-truth I'd given him.

Staying vigilant, I didn't dare to lift the mask from my face and expose any feelings I had for Emilia. I couldn't risk the FBI pulling me from this case; more was at stake now.

After briefly pondering my explanation, he bent low, so he was at eye level.

"What a sweet job you must have. I have to abide by the law, but she is a sexy woman. What I'd give to have a go at the sweet cunt of hers ..." he admits, a malicious glint flickering in his eyes as he looks down at the video in his hands. I flared my nostrils at his candor, not wanting this asshole to get off to the sight of her. I wanted to break every bone in his face until he was unrecognizable. He continued on, jarring me from my murderous thoughts. "But, if Emilia opening her legs for you gets her to open up to you, then so be it. Fuck her until she submits."

Breathe in, *one, two, three,* breathe out.

With cold determination in my voice, I gave him the answer he wanted to hear from me.

"Consider it done."

After Tobias had used his knife to release me from the makeshift cuffs, I wasted no time sticking around to hear anything he had to say. If he wanted to talk to me, he knew how to reach me. Right now, I was in no mood to talk. Right now, I wanted to punch someone to a bloody pulp. I wanted to feel the thick, sticky sensation of someone else's blood streaming through my fingers. Running couldn't push this beast inside my chest down. I needed to expel this pent-up energy I had crawling beneath my skin. I ran back toward the city with a destination in mind. If I couldn't beat the shit out of anyone, well, I'll settle for getting my anger out in a more healthy way—behind the walls of a shooting range.

When I got to the shooting range that I liked to frequent, it was ominously silent. Even during the slow hours of the morning, there were always at least one or two other people here. Something was off when I walked into the waiting area. I noticed that even the workers weren't behind the desk like they were supposed to be. I reached behind me, grabbing my gun from my back holster and raised it. I silently moved closer to the gun range, my senses on overdrive. Upon entering the firing range, I heard the distinct sounds of a gun being fired off rapidly. Whoever it was hadn't heard me come in with their headgear on, and I used that to my advantage as I followed the sound. To my complete surprise, I found myself staring down at a woman in a tight green skirt and a white halter top, revealing her snake tattoo.

CHAPTER EIGHTEEN

EMILIA

THE GUNSHOTS REVERBERATED INSIDE THE METAL DIVIDE I WAS in as I repeatedly pulled the trigger and aimed it at the target twenty-five yards down the line. I smelled the sulfur in the air, and the scent grounded me where I stood.

I had tossed and turned half the night, barely getting any rest because of what had transpired between me and Matteo. *My bodyguard.* I had to remind myself of that fact. He wasn't someone I could flaunt around town as a piece of eye candy like I did with others. There was a fine line between us, and we didn't just step over the line last night, we bulldozed through it. Now that line was blurred and my body and my mind were at war over it.

I knew it was reckless to have gotten involved with him. This line of work was dangerous, and attachments, whether emotional or physical, were careless. Yet, my body craved more. Being who I was, I had to remain calm, collected and in control twenty-four seven. But with him I felt wild and free. I liked being dominated by Matteo. Giving up control in the bedroom was unheard of for me. With past partners, I was always the one in charge and had to explain to the men what I wanted, but Matteo just knew what I needed. He forced it out of me, piece by piece. And I would never admit it out loud to him, but I knew he had ruined me for future partners.

My frustration led me here, to a safe space. I needed to regain my control, and I knew this was the way to do it. I felt powerful with the weight of my 9mm perfectly enclosed in my hands. I loaded a new magazine in and raised my arms once more as I fired at the target. Eighteen shots later, I pushed the button to bring my target closer for inspection. Five shots through the head, five shots pierced the target where the heart would be, and eight more directly through the center of the chest. A smile fell upon my face as I held the paper target in my hand. All those years of training, all those years of captivity, I'd vowed that when I was free again, I would never let myself be unguarded, vulnerable. My father trusted the wrong family; he let his guard down, and it cost him everything, his life included. I would never allow them to have me again.

The security that the *Septem Daemonia* could offer me weighed heavily on my mind. I knew I had to make a decision, and soon. They wouldn't wait forever for my response. I tried to compare the pros and cons of the secret society, and to be quite frank, I was only coming up with more pros. *So why amI hesitating to give them my answer?*

My body perked up then at the words of the man that stood behind me.

"Not a bad shot," he said, sidling up behind me. He was close enough that I could smell his cologne, a smoky vanilla and bergamot mixed in with sweat. He ran the tips of his fingers down my exposed arms, making goosebumps rise in his wake. He knew exactly what he was doing to me, as I let my body win over my mind and I dropped my head back onto his chest.

His other hand splayed out on my waist, right below my top. The halter top I had on was tied up by my neck, exactly where he was trailing kisses. He whispered into my ear, low and raspy, "Have you missed me, *il mio diavolessa?*"* At his words, I could feel the wetness in between my thighs, and in the position I was in from firing my gun, my legs were already spread wide for him. Judging by his growing length behind me, he liked it too.

"Not in the slightest," I lied, moving to put my gun down on the small bench before me.

He tsked at my movement.

"Keep it," he ordered me. "I like seeing violence on you, it's turning me on and it's only fair I do the same to you." He grabbed my gun and loaded it with new bullets. Once he did, he handed it to me, his words finally sinking in.

"Let's see how good of a shot you are when you're ..." He unties the knot at my neck and the straps fall forward exposing my breasts to the cold air."... distracted," he finished, pinching my peaked nipple for effect.

"You can't be serious," I deadpanned, the want for him increasing between my legs. I had never done this before, and the sensation of his words and what he wanted to do was a huge fucking turn-on. It was a win-win situation for me. I was remaining in power, while also being stripped of it, and I was soaked by that discovery.

His hand on my waist slipped lower as I felt him lift the hem of my skirt higher, and when he sunk a finger between my folds and felt how much this turned me on, he finally answered.

I tasted myself on his finger as he thrust it in between my lips and I sucked on him greedily.

"Deadly," he enunciated slowly. "Now pull the damn trigger, *principessa.*"

And with those words, he thrust his fingers back inside my wet cunt, his other hand kneading my breasts into submission. God, I'd never been so turned on in my life. I couldn't func-

---

* Gangsta - Kehlani

tion; my body was overwhelmed and the sensations he was pulling from my body transported me into another dimension. My body felt loose, like I'd been drugged, and I leaned back into him for support. I got lost in the way he played my pussy like an instrument he'd perfected. I was on the cusp of an orgasm already, when he pulled his fingers from my body.

"You don't get to finish, Emilia, not until you fire your weapon," he reprimanded me, gripping my chin in his hands so I peered upwards at him. "Now tell me, are you going to be a good girl for me? Because if so, then I'll let you come all over my fingers."

My body trembled in his arms as I nodded.

"I want your words," he scolded, digging in harder.

"Yes," I stuttered. "Yes, I'll be good."

I took a deep breath, as much as I could muster, and I raised my gun and aimed. I pulled the trigger right as he resumed pulling the orgasm from my body. I could barely focus on the target in front of me as I continued to aim and fire, while he continued his ruthless onslaught between my legs.

I fired off another shot as my orgasm crested, my chest engulfed in fire as it consumed me. My chest heaved in his grasp and I felt like my body was on fire. On impulse, I started to shift my legs closer together, but he stepped forward, placing both his feet in between my legs and thrusting them back out. I felt the tingling sensation of my orgasm throughout my body and I didn't just want it, I needed the release.

I fired another bullet.

Two more bullets were left in the chamber.

"When that last bullet is fired, then you are finally allowed to come, Emilia. You come before the last bullet, and there will be consequences," he directed me.

I fired another bullet, as I bit down hard on my lip at the intense orgasm fighting its way through my body. I didn't even know at that point if my shots were true, but as I fired my last bullet, my orgasm ripped me to shreds as I succumbed to the immense pleasure that rushed through my body. I felt everything with such intensity with my legs spread open like that. He drew out my orgasm with his fingers, playing with my clit as I rode out the feeling. He spun me around and slammed me back into the table, my gun clattering to the ground.

"Now, you can have your reward."

I didn't have time to answer him as his mouth replaced his fingers, and he lapped me up like I was his last meal. He pulled one of my legs onto his shoulder, and sucked my clit into his mouth, biting down hard. I cried out his name, wanting more, needing more. And he obliged. He took it all, everything I gave, and I grabbed his head and brought him closer to my sex, needing to feel the friction of his beard on my pussy. And when I did, I detonated once more in his mouth, and I crumbled before him.

He wasted no time after that. In that next moment, he had my legs wrapped around his body, and my skirt high above my waist. My pussy soaked his shirt, until I was ripping it off him in one fell swoop. I felt the warmth emanating from his body, as I drank his tattoos in. Drank him in. Splattered across his naked torso was a collage of artwork. In my brief glimpses, I caught an eagle, a cross and a skull, but I didn't have time to appreciate his body before I felt his cock split me open. He fucked me hard against the metal barrier table, my spine bruising in the process. I dug my nails deeper into his back, pulling him as close as I could get.

He had no idea what he'd just done for me at that moment. He may have taken away my power sexually, yet he still allowed me to be in control. I wasn't left exposed, but rather remained the one in power. And that left me in a fugue-like state. I was on cloud nine, and with every thrust inside me, I became more turned on. His hands left imprints where they;d latched on to my thighs and I secretly hoped he branded me in such a way.

"Fuck, Emilia. You feel incredible!" he growled into my ear, before taking my lips in an aggressive kiss. With every thrust inside my body, I sunk deeper and deeper into that blissful state, drowning in that sensation. I didn't dare come up for air, because I knew when I did, it would be over.

"Matteo!" I screamed out his name, as he hit a spot that made me liquify in his arms. "Fuck, it's too much," I whimpered. "You're too much."

The orgasms that he drew from my body caused my clit to be over-sensitive, and the brush of every thrust felt like I was going to combust.

"You can take it," he implored.

My head fell back, and the wave of my orgasm flooded my senses. I cried out, right as he dipped and tugged on my nipple, and I fell apart right there in his arms.

"I got you, *principessa*," he murmured inches from my lips. "Let go."

I didn't need to be asked twice. I unleashed it all, and he took it, releasing his own pleasure inside me, and slowly he bent his knees, bringing us down to the floor.*

Satiated and blissed out, I lazily went to pull at my straps, when he covered my hand and shook his head. He gently pushed my hair to the side of my neck and began to tie my top back into place.

He cradled my head in his hands, staring at me wordlessly, and I wondered if he was going to say anything, but he didn't. He sat like that with me for at least a few minutes, before he let out a long sigh and guided me to a standing position with him.

"Let's see how good your aim was when you were distracted," he teased me with a sly smirk.

---

* Stop playing Gangsta - Kehlani

I took a step forward on trembling legs toward the metal table. I pushed the button, starting the mechanism that brought the target closer, and together we analyzed my shots.

"I'm impressed, Emilia. Even with my fingers buried inside that sweet cunt of yours, you still managed to hit vital organs," he chuckled. "Remind me to never piss you off."

He slid a hand around my body, and I glanced down to see he had my gun, the nozzle pointed down the lane.

"I have been underestimated by men all my life—I've gotten used to it," I said coldly, bitterness dripping from every word. I started to rack the magazine once more with bullets, when I felt him place his hand on my waist.

"I never underestimated you, Emilia. I simply just wanted to challenge you in unprecedented ways." He spread his fingers wider on my waist, where my skin was exposed. "I pity the fool who dares try to underestimate you. I have a feeling it'll be the last thing they do."

I stifled a shiver that ran through my body at his touch on my skin. I defused the tension between us by trying to change the topic.

"You're learning, Mr. Ricci."

His touch disappeared at my words.

"Back to formalities I see, Miss DeLuca," he said, setting up next to me in the next station with his own Glock.

I side-eyed him, puzzled.

"What?"

"Do I need to be making you come in order for you to scream my name? Because, if that is the case, then challenge accepted. I guess I will just need to keep putting myself between your legs more often."

My mouth fell open slightly at his bold statement.

"I did tell you to use me." He smirked over at me, racking the slide back, locking the first bullet into place. "I intend to return the favor."

Before I could answer him, he'd already fired down the shooting lane.

"Let's make this interesting, *principessa*."

He laid his gun down on the table and turned to me then, his body leaning up against the metal barrier between us.

"We'll play a game," he started. "I call an area on the target, you shoot it. You deviate from my precise location, you tell me something about you."

"And if I hit the mark?"

"I will tell you whatever you want to know about me."

I pretended to ponder over his request, bating him with my answer.

"You got yourself a deal. Same rules apply to you."

He nodded his head in answer and we began, taking turns. He informed me it should be ladies first, so I readied myself into position. I racked my magazine and released the slide, chambering the round.

I lifted my arms at the target, my pointer finger just hovering off the side of the barrel of the gun.

"Left eye socket," he fired off.

I moved my finger, and squeezed the trigger. The gun ejected the bullet, and I saw when it ripped straight through the target, dead center through the left eye socket.

Keeping the barrel of the gun aimed toward the target, I looked over at Matteo, where I found a warm, relaxed smile had reached his eyes, creating crinkles at the corners.

He's got dimples, how fucking cute.

"What made you start your own gun-for-hire contracting business?" I pressed him.

His smile faltered a bit, but not fully.

"After I departed from the military, the thing I craved the most was my autonomy. When I was in the navy, I followed orders even if I wholeheartedly disagreed with them. Or the way they went about things. I was a soldier, another number to the United States. But they made me into a killer, whether I wanted to be or not. And I was *fucking* good at it," he stated matter-of-factly. "So, I decided to create my own company. My men and I do things that government agencies can't do because they abide by the law, we *bend* the law so to speak. We go places beyond our country's limitations and we get the job done discreetly. In and out, no evidence."

He stopped, waiting to hear my response. Waiting to see if I'd judge him. The thing he didn't know is that I understood him completely. We were one and the same. Both turned into soldiers, trained to kill. Neither one of us followed the law, but merely bent the rules to play in our favor. Only difference was, he had a choice. I didn't. I felt obligated to keep the DeLuca family name and its legacy running. All I had known from a young age was pain and violence, and those who were loyal to my father paid for it in blood. After Romeo had violated me way too many times and disposed of me, that still haunted me to this day. I vowed I'd take up the family name once more and enact my revenge.

"Playing by the rules is overrated anyways," I replied.

His smile came back in full force then, and I was taken aback briefly at the sight of it, because Matteo Ricci was absolutely beautiful when he smiled.

"Duly noted." Matteo laughed, and I thought it might be one of my favorite sounds.

"My turn," I responded. "But I want you to shoot with your non-dominant hand. The right ear," I said flirtatiously.

He shook with laughter as he smiled coyly over at me. "That's cute, Emilia."

He aimed his Glock45 down at his target and pulled the trigger, and I held my breath, the anticipation killing me because I knew I'd found my match. I was naturally competitive, or maybe it was the Leo in me, but I had a sense that Matteo was just as competitive. I peered around the corner of the barrier and exhaled a long sigh.

"Open up, *principessa*."

The double meaning didn't slip by me.

"How did you do it?" His voice was stern, serious.

I cocked my head to the side, puzzled at the question.

"How did I do what?"

"How did you kill your husband, Romeo Morelli?"

I took a step back as he stepped closer to me, caging me up against the metal barrier.

"Wh-Why are you asking me that?" I stuttered up at him. He was standing so close to me that I had to tilt my head backward to look at him.

"Because I want to make sure that you made it hurt. That you made him suffer in his last moments. You said the same rules apply. Answer the question, Emilia," he ordered, tilting my chin up higher so that I felt the strain in my neck. He was going to make this hurt if I didn't answer truthfully. Not even Dante knew the full story as to what happened to Romeo. All he knew was that I had taken care of the issue, that it was handled. Was I really going to let this man, this stranger, know those intimate details of that part of my life? I hesitated, but a part of me felt like I could tell Matteo the truth. That'd he listen and be accepting of the person that I had become at that time.

"Yes, I made him suffer," I confessed under my breath.

His hand cupped my face as he leaned down to whisper, "Tell me all about it."

My eyes darted to the green pools of his eyes and I searched them, but he looked genuine, not malicious.

"My ex-husband liked to purchase whores, even when he was married to me," I began. "In a way, his disposal of me was his biggest mistake because he thought he had seen the last of me. But, much to his surprise, the *whore* he had hired that night was me. I made sure it would be his last.

"I was already in the room when he arrived, dressed in cherry red, his favorite color. He preferred redheads, so I made sure to wear a wig, so he wouldn't recognize me at first.

Upon entering, I put on the charm and forced him to lay on the bed. He liked it kinky," I explained to Matteo. "I tied his hands and feet to the bedpost, and gagged him with one of the toys I knew he was preparing to use on me that night. And just when I sat down on his naked body, and he peered up at me, I saw his eyes flicker with confusion, then absolute terror when I removed the wig and he released the monster he had willingly allowed into his bed.

"Have you heard of death by a thousand cuts?" I asked Matteo, pulling away from my story. He simply nodded at my question, and I watched his throat move as he swallowed in response, the sound of his heartbeat increasing rapidly.

"Are you scared, Mr. Ricci?"

*"On the contrary, Miss DeLuca, I am absolutely turned on by this violent streak of yours. Do continue," he pleaded.

I smiled wickedly at him as I proceeded with my story.

"He struggled under my weight, but he wasn't going anywhere. And no guards would come looking for him either, because I knew how rough he liked to be with his women, and that he wanted no interruption or witnesses. So, he knew no help would come for him. I watched as the hope in his eyes died at that realization. And then I took my time crafting my masterpiece."

Matteo leaned down and nibbled on my ear, his fingers finding their way to their new home, between my legs.

"You're soaked, baby," he informed me. "Does violence turn you on too, *il mio diavolessa*?"

He didn't wait for a response as his hand spread my legs further, giving him more access to my wet heat.

"Then what did you do?" he questioned, between biting and sucking on my neck.

"I ... I took a knife and carved him up. 1,522 slices to his body, one for every day I spent in hell. One for every day I

---

* Continue playing Gangsta - Kehlani

wanted to die holed up there, but not before I got my revenge. I held out long enough to make it to that moment to show him that he had failed in killing me. He may have killed my innocence and the hope that burned bright inside that young, naive girl, but because of his decision, I was able to rise up from the ashes like a phoenix and make him choke on it." My story cut off at the sudden gasp I let out at the feel of his fingers inside me. The feelings that arose in me from his touch had me squirming beneath his weight, wanting more of him even though every movement was almost too much.

I wrapped my arms around his neck and shamelessly ground my pussy hard on his hand, swirling my hips to make sure I hit just the right spot. When his thumb pressed down on my swollen clit, I buckled in his grasp, my arms going slack.

"Keep going," he moaned into my mouth, sucking on my tongue with fervor.

He twisted his thumb, sending a jolt of pleasure through my body that momentarily left me breathless.

"I sliced away skin, layer by layer. I left marks all over his body to the point that when I was done carving him up, there was no surface area for me to cut into, it was just his blood. I sat there on top of him in lingerie the same color, enjoying the view I had of him bleeding out slowly and painfully at my hands.

"I remember sitting there, waiting for the moment when the light would leave his eyes when I thought to myself, I had come full circle. My marriage with Romeo had started off with blood between my legs and it was ending with blood once more between my legs, the only difference was that it was his blood this time."

I moaned into his neck, as he continued to worship my body in all the ways I needed. He crooked his fingers inside me, and his name fell from my lips in a plea. A plea to make me come, to fuck me, to do whatever he wanted to me.

"I ... I ..." I tried to get out, but his movements had my

whole body trembling from the oncoming orgasm that I knew was escalating inside. I was almost there when he slowed down his movements, sending my impending orgasm away.

"What are you doing? Don't stop, Matteo," I begged, not even caring if that made me seem needy.

"There's more to the story, finish it and maybe I'll let you finish."

I let out a heavy breath, daggers in my eyes that he must have found charming, because he simply laughed and lazily played with my sex just shy of where I wanted him.

With an eye roll, I finished my story. "Right as he took his last breath, I leaned down and whispered in his ear the person that I'd become was someone he had made. That my undoing was his reckoning, and I shoved my knife between his ribs and pierced his heart."

Matteo started up once more, adding more pressure and increasing his speed. He added a third finger and the feeling of being stretched wide by him had me throwing my head back in ecstasy, as I tried to finish the story quickly.

"I didn't bother cleaning up afterwards, I walked right out of that house covered in his blood and in skimpy lingerie, right as the flames began to devour what was left of Romeo Morelli.

"MATTEO!" I cried, wanting more of him. I wanted him to fill me up, to make me his whore, his princess, whatever the fuck he wanted me to be. I wanted to take him up on that offer of using him. In all honesty, I wanted him to use me up in whatever way he liked. I reveled in pain, and when pleasure was part of that mix, it was like an addiction.

"You're so pretty when you come," he confessed, catching my moan in his mouth. Our tongues battled for dominance, and he pulled back, almost as breathless as I was.*

"I don't know what he put you through, but I can see the

---

* Stop playing Gangsta - Kehlani

haunted look in your eyes. I see it a lot in the eyes of men in the military, so I'm glad that bastard got what he deserved. *Black Widow* seems very fitting, indeed." He pulled his fingers from between my legs and brought them to his lips. He let his fingers rest on his bottom lip, not taking his fingers inside his mouth, but they sat there as his tongue darted out to get a taste of my juices. He forced them inside my mouth then when he saw my eyes blown wide with lust. I sucked on his fingers, my cheeks hollowing out, as he forced them deeper.

"You like the way you taste, *principessa*?"

I nodded greedily, licking the rest of myself off hungrily.

"Without looking, aim at his heart," he instructed me. I didn't have to ask him who the *him* part of that sentence was supposed to be. I kept my eyes locked on his as I picked up my gun with my right hand and aimed. Instincts took over , and I knew exactly where to position my weapon before I pulled the trigger. I didn't bother looking at the target swaying, the smug grin inching its way across my face as I watched Matteo's expression shift to defeat, but pride lingered behind his eyes.

"Fair enough, Emilia. Ask your question."

I thought long and hard about what I wanted to ask him. What secret I wanted him to divulge to me. He didn't hold back with Romeo, so neither would I. I thought back to when I did my background check on him, and remembered seeing a mission that was blacked out beside the name.

"Tell me about Operation Blackstone?"

The second the words left my lips, I knew I was going to regret it. Matteo stumbled backward as if I had shot him. His gun shook in his hand by his side, and he got a faraway look in his eyes. As if he was reliving that mission. I reached out to touch him, to apologize, but he reared back, his eyes wide as if just noticing I was still there.

"How do you know about Operation Blackstone? That is classified information." He demanded, grabbing my arm roughly.

How quickly his touch of pleasure morphed into that of pain.

I pried his fingers off my arm and took a calculated step back, putting myself into an offensive position in case he decided to attack. Matteo's face channeled so many emotions, it was difficult to keep track of what he was feeling, from shock to anger to numbness. I watched as he shut down right in front of me. Those walls he'd started to let down earlier, they were rising back up, taller and reinforced with something stronger. He was shutting me out, and I found myself disappointed. Disappointed I had laid it out on the line for him, dug up skeletons from my past, but he couldn't offer me the same in return.

"It was in the background check. No information, just a name. I was curious," I tried, but he wasn't having it.

"Don't be curious, don't be anything," he shouted, causing me to put more space between us.

"This was a mistake," he mumbled to himself.

"Same rules apply, Matteo. Answer the question," I threw his own words back at him, praying that he would give me an inch. But instead he looked me in the eyes with such a deadly expression on his face.

"Playing by the rules is overrated anyways," he taunted back at me, slicing me to my core with his rejection. And with those parting words, he turned and left me alone again in the gun range.

Pissed off, I fired the rest of the bullets in my gun at the target in frustration, all hitting their mark in one giant hole— through the heart.

CHAPTER NINETEEN

MATTEO

I CRUMBLED INTO PIECES TODAY IN FRONT OF EMILIA, WHICH I was not proud of. Her question had thrown me off balance and I let it get the best of me. My day had started out like shit with the betrayal of Tobias and Emilia had distracted me. She temporarily put my mind and heart at ease when I was in her presence. That doesn't happen often to me, not after the military. I'd allowed SSA Richards' words to get to me, and I'd needed to blow off some steam. Going to the shooting range was the only healthy way for me to do that.

Imagine my surprise when I'd found Emilia had the same bright ideas as I had. It was fun torturing and teasing her. Making her squirm under my touch, knowing I was the one that made her moan like that, that a simple touch from me could make her fold and open up to me in more ways than I had imagined.

I was enthralled with everything Emilia, and every minute with her had eased the tension that had been building in my shoulders since I had left the van. I wanted to get her out of her comfort zone, and she did just that. My distraction game made her putty in my hands and my dick hard. I wasn't lying to the FBI when I'd said intimacy was the way to get her to reveal her secrets. I was a master at making women fall for my charm, and she was no exception. Except, in a way, she was. She challenged me right back with her mysterious allure. She had a magnetism about her, an aura about her that just pulled you in by your balls, until it was you that fell on your knees before her.

She was my equal; watching her in action with her gun was thrilling, and she matched me in that department, shot for shot. Even though my intent had been to distract her, she'd had me transfixed from the start. From the second my hand was between her legs, I was distracted from everything else around me. I simply forgot who I was supposed to be when I was around her, and I was flirting with a dangerous line.

The more intimate I got with Emilia, the more she opened up to me, and I'd learned something new about her. Even though my fingers had her momentarily preoccupied, my ears were hanging on to every word that fell from her lips. The way she took her life back from her shitty ex-husband was mesmerizing. I wasn't entirely sure what had happened to Emilia in those missing years, but it was something bad to have left her with that faraway haunted look in those blue eyes of hers. Her ice-blue eyes were so cold when she'd told her story that they reminded me of icebergs.

Most icebergs were submerged in water. The part of the iceberg that floated above the water, that was the part people saw, but below the water, the hidden parts, that was where you found the secrets, the skeletons, the trauma. In order to find those, you had to be willing to go deeper, below the surface. Emilia reminded me of that. She had all these layers to her, that no one knew. She came off as a powerful woman in a den of hungry men. Chicago was a city filled with mafia culture, it was a man's world that she'd boldly inserted herself into with her head held high.

She was riveting to witness firsthand. She did not bend or break for any man, and her story was a testament to that. She fed the beast inside her and became the monster she needed to be after the men in her life had all disappointed her.

*All was well, until she'd hit me right back with the personal questions. How Operation Blackstone even came up in her background check was beyond me. That mission should have been expunged from all records. I knew firsthand that the US government would never want the general public to know the dirty and albeit illegal operation they had their soldiers commit under the false pretense of war and for the freedom of America. Those five words had gutted me. *Tell me about Operation Blackstone.* How could I tell her about the military operation that made me question our government, that made me into a person I can no longer stand to look at in the mirror? A man that should've died alongside his brethren and the innocent.

I didn't want to tell her about that operation because, legally, I couldn't. It didn't exist, and if she knew the full story it could get her killed. And I would rather relive that day all over again than have Emilia's blood on my hands. I may struggle with the decisions I'd had to make at that time, but I was not going to throw that baggage onto Emilia's shoulders.

I lay on my bed, undeserving of the luxuries that I was awarded while my brothers remained buried six feet under in an undisclosed location. Caskets were buried back here in the States, but their bodies weren't inside. There were no bodies to bring home.

Exhaustion took me under, but I couldn't sleep, I was plagued by nightmares.†

I could smell the burning bodies around me as our humvee rattled down the empty street. It was too quiet for this neighborhood, and my men and I were on high alert. I sat in the passenger seat of the first of the two vehicles that were sent over. My gut told me something was off, but I was

---

* Haunted - Kane Brown, Jelly Roll
† Stop playing Haunted - Kane Brown, Jelly Roll

not in command. I took orders and that was it. I was merely a soldier in this war. Black smoke billowed around us from cars that were on fire, cloaking the town in ash. Stray dogs roamed the streets, scrounging for their next meal, paying no attention to the men in uniforms with machine guns.

Our order was to search a town for a suspect in a bombing a few weeks back. Intel had come from one of our own trusted CIs, but this looked more like a ghost town to me. Houses looked abandoned from the street, but then again American troops weren't exactly welcomed here, and most of the civilians stayed in their houses rather than interact with us.

Landon was driving the vehicle, going on about his fiance, Hannah, and that they'd finally set a date for their wedding.

"She wants a June wedding," he told us. "She's practically picked everything out, from flowers, music, vendors, to even the seating arrangements. Do men not have a say in these things anymore?"

Tobias perks up from the back, grabbing the headrest in front.

"Guys never had a say in anything wedding-related. All you have to do is show up; that's just the way it goes."

Laughter filled the truck at Landon's disappointment over not partaking in any of the wedding plans.

"Well, I—"

But, Landon never got to finish his sentence because it was then that our truck hit an IUD and the next thing I knew, the vehicle was being catapulted into the air and slammed back down on its side. That's when the gunfire started to rain down on our vehicles. My side was up in the air, and I turned in my seat to take a headcount of my men. They were injured like I was, but breathing for the moment. I turned back to check in on Landon, but his head fell at an unusual angle. I choked back a sob that wanted to rip its way up my throat. I felt his neck for a pulse, but my friend was gone, his neck snapped.

I learned real quick that the intel given to us was an ambush, and I had a funny feeling that our command knew what we were walking into.

My men sprang into action, exiting the vehicle and returning fire on our enemy. I followed suit, my unit heading to the nearest shelter in an abandoned building not occupied by the enemy.

They picked us off one by one.

Johnny went down first, a bullet to the neck. He was a father of two, with another baby on the way. A baby girl that he would never get to meet.

Sam was the last one to fall. He took three bullets to the chest shielding myself and Tobias. He and his wife were hoping to start a family soon; they had only been married two years.

Tobias fell after a knife in his abdomen, but he survived because I got us out in time to get him medical help. But not without the sacrifice of my men.

My men had taken down six of our enemies, while the other unit laid down fire covering us.

*Operation Blackstone had lasted a total of twenty-nine minutes.

Twenty-nine minutes for me to lose my soul.

Twenty-nine minutes to watch three of my brothers die needlessly.

Twenty-nine minutes that altered my life forever.

Those were twenty-nine minutes I could never get back. And if I could I would have told my commanding officer no. If I had only questioned the mission, my brothers would be alive, and I wouldn't feel like my hands were stained with their blood.

Their deaths were on me. As their Captain, it was me that had led them on that mission. I'd failed them from the start. Every night I battled, replaying that operation over and over again, crafting alternate scenarios in my head in hopes they'd lead to a different result. The results were the same: I woke up from night terrors and my brothers were still dead. Then when I was awake, I faced down my demons head-on, because I remained breathing, alive, and they didn't.

That day I lost my brothers, but those women lost a fiancé, a husband, a father.

I was unmarried, had no one to mourn me after my death

---

* Continue playing Haunted - Kane Brown. Jelly Roll

besides my brothers in arms. So, I battled with that on my conscience, because why was I worth saving that day, but they weren't?

I tossed and turned in my bed, having one-sided conversations with ghosts before I finally relented and made a rash decision. The only thing that was going to keep me grounded was the very thing that I was trying so hard to avoid.

Before I changed my mind, I rushed out of my room and already had my hand raised, knocking on hers. I begged God that she would open the door for me, because while God may be forgiving, Emilia DeLuca wasn't.

CHAPTER TWENTY

EMILIA

I FELT LIKE I WAS ONE OF THOSE OLD-SCHOOL PINBALL machines, and my heart was the pinball. One minute I was enjoying Matteo's company, dropping my guard around him and ultimately having a good time. I was laughing for the first time in a long time. Cut to now, hours later, with an irritated bodyguard across the hall.

Had I crossed the line asking him that question?

No, I didn't think so. Why was he allowed to ask me personal questions about my past, but I wasn't able to ask the same of him?

I paced my bedroom, leaving marks on the carpet. I toyed with the idea of dismissing Matteo altogether. Out of sight, out of mind and that whole spiel. But I was selfish. I knew I couldn't let him go because I needed him. Despite his mood swings, he made me feel alive, more than I'd ever felt before. I knew he would open up to me; it would just take time.

I sank onto my duvet, my black silk slip coming up to mid-thigh as I leaned forward, bringing my head into my hands.

How did I get myself into this position?

Just as my thoughts started to drift into self-sabotaging mode, a series of knocks sounded on my door.

I crossed my room to find a disheveled Matteo braced against my door frame, his hands clutching the frame above him in a death grip.

"I can't tell you specifics about Operation Blackstone, because legally it doesn't exist, and you knowing that name puts your life in danger," he blurts, his fingers flexing on the wood as if he wanted to rip it into pieces. "But I can tell you that I lost really good men on that op, and their deaths haunt me when I sleep and follow me like a shadow through the day. It tears me apart from the inside out, and I can't stop the voices that are in my head, but you"—he looks head on at me, finally making contact—"but you quiet the demons in my head."

His hands let go of the wood frame above him and instead he holds onto the edges of the door, as if they are his crutch.

"You quiet the noise. With you, I don't think about them or that night. With you, I can breathe again." He stumbled over his words, his Adam's apple bobbing in his throat like the words were painful to admit.

"Please help me quiet the voices, Emilia."

I pulled him into my room, and he used that to reach out and take my face in his hands.

He kissed me and it was a jumble of tongues and unsaid apologies.

We fumbled over one another until my bare legs hit the edge of my bed, and he guided me down, towering over me.

I hadn't realized in his rambling confession that he had come to my room in only his boxer briefs.

This man that stood over me like an Adonis was so beautiful it hurt. For the first time, I truly took in Matteo Ricci.

His hair was cropped short to his head, but there was this one strand that fell loosely right over his forehead, and just kind of dangled over his left eyebrow. He gazed down at me like I was a long-lost dream he'd once had, his green eyes shining like emeralds in the sun. His chiseled jawline, simply put, was art, as if a sculptor had created him from scratch or the bones of a God. Then there were his tattoos. They crawled up every surface of his body, no skin untouched besides his face. No, I'm glad he had left that to be a master-piece of its own creation.

"Use me, Matteo, in whichever way you'd like. I'm here," I consoled him, reaching up to trace the hidden scar beneath one of his tattoos on his chest. "Let me turn down the voices in your head."

A small flicker of hope resonated behind his eyes, and more than anything I wanted to help make this broken man whole again.

"To my heart's desire?" He cocked his head, questioning.

"To your heart's desire," I confirmed.

*He lifted himself off the bed and made his way onto the chaise lounge in the corner of my bedroom. I sat up in bed, moving to stand and make my way over to him, when his dominance made its presence known.

"Crawl to me," he demanded.

He repeated himself when I didn't make a move.

"On your hands and knees, Emilia, and crawl to me."

I sank slowly to my knees, feeling the heat between my legs already at being ordered around by him. The stern directness in his tone had my toes curling.

---

* Sacrifice (feat. Jessie Reyes) - Black Atlass, Jessie Reyez

I crawled to him slowly, my breasts spilling over my negligee, and I watched as he bit down on his knuckles before wetting his lips.

He palmed his cock as I crawled to sit right at his feet.

"On your feet."

I followed his instructions, curious to see what he'd demand from me next.

He pulled me in by the back of my thighs, and spun me around in one quick move. His hands coasted over my skin teasingly, the barest touch of him driving me crazy, as he skimmed past my sex with his knuckles.

"Take these off."

He lifted my slip up so my ass was eye level with him, and leaned forward and bit down hard before releasing and smacking it. I took my time torturing him back, hooking my fingers underneath the sheer black string and gliding it down my legs until it hit the floor.

He turned me around to face him, and even though I was looking down at him from a position of power, there was no doubt who was in complete control here.

"Now put them in your mouth."

I bit at my lip, not quite understanding.

"Did I stutter, Emilia? Put your panties in your mouth. We can't have your guards hearing how pretty you sound when I make you scream my name."

I didn't have to run my fingers through my slit to know how turned on I was right now. I bent down and grabbed my panties off the floor and put them in my mouth, tasting my essence.

"Now tell me, Emilia, are you going to be a whore for me tonight?

"Yes," I mumbled through the fabric.

"That's a good girl."

He stood up, brushing past me for my nightstand before pulling out my drawer filled with my toys, a gleam in his eye.

"How naughty of you. Shall I use these on you?" he asked.

I nodded eagerly, begging him silently with my eyes to touch me already. I could feel my skin crawling in anticipation.

"Sit on the bed and spread your legs for me," his next order came.

I made my way back to my bed, my back resting against the headboard, and I slowly spread my legs as he crawled between them.

"That's a good little slut. Now, keep those legs spread wide, baby. I want to see every inch of you when I make you come."

And with no warning, he thrust one of my toys inside me. He used my toy ruthlessly on me, never relenting. I grabbed a fistful of my sheets in my hands and when he turned the vibrations to the highest level, I panted unashamedly, grinding my pussy back into him, greedy for more.

"Are you going to take my cock like this, naughty girl? Your cunt is so wet, all ready for me. How many times did you want me to make you come? Twice? Three times? Or as much as I tell you to?"

"Repeatedly," I tried to say through the fabric.

"On your knees and keep those legs spread. Fuck, that's a good girl," he coaxed me, moving my vibrator to my clit. Just as my orgasm peaked and ripped through my body, he slipped my anal beads inside me from behind using the lubricant from between my legs.

"Holy fucking God," I mumbled.

"Don't pray to him, *il mio diavolessa*, he can't help you. One of these days, Emilia, I'm going to take this sweet ass of yours and I'm going to make you my filthy whore. Tell me, would you like that? Would you like me breaking you open in that way?" he asked, running his fingers through my slick folds.

"Mmm," I managed to muster between coming down

from my orgasm high and feeling the sensations of the beads working inside me.

He ripped my slip down my body, grabbing a fistful of my ass in his hand.

"Fuck, Emilia, what are you doing to me?" he asked.

He flipped me over so I was on my back and pulled the makeshift gag out of my mouth.

"Now suck," he commanded, hovering over my mouth.

He didn't need to give me any further instruction. I licked my lips at his growing erection inside his boxer briefs and hastily removed the obstacle in my way. I looked at his cock like I was a starved woman, and part of me was.

I took his length into my mouth, hollowing out my cheeks to accommodate for his size, and I licked, sucked, and swirled my tongue over his shaft and balls.

"Fuck, Emilia!" Matteo moaned. "You truly are the devil."

I repeated this over and over again, until I felt his legs tense under my hands and I braced for the hot liquid that poured down the back of my throat and I swallowed down every last drop he had to give.

He wiped the last of his come on my lips, pushing the rest into my mouth.

"Swallow."

I licked at my lips, tasting the saltiness on my tongue.

He pulled me up off the bed and led me by the hand to my balcony.

"Matteo, what are you doing?"

"I have an idea," he said, not elaborating much further than those four simple words. My balcony looked over the back of the estate, where the gardens and inground pool with the bar in the middle were located. My balcony was perched high, so my bodyguards couldn't technically see me, unless they were further out in the gardens, which they would be in fifteen minutes.

Matteo pinned my naked body up against the railings of

my balcony, the cold sensation sparking an excitement in me at the sudden difference in temperature from my heated skin. He wrapped his arm under my leg and gently placed it down on top of the railing. The position not only spread me wide open, but puts me on full display should anyone happen to look up.

"This is my pussy," he stated, slapping my ass, the movement pushing me further into the railings, causing friction on my clit.

"Fuck yes, Matteo."

I heard rather than saw him drop down to his knees.

And then the next minute Matteo's tongue was thrusting inside my pussy, and the angle had me whimpering and begging for more. He pushed the anal beads deeper inside me, twisting them and turning them different ways and I felt the tingle shoot through my body as he ate me from behind, and I'd never felt so powerful splayed out on display like that.

I bit down on my lip to keep from screaming his name too loud, but I couldn't stop the moans that tore their way out of my throat.

"You're soaking my face, Emilia, fuck, baby."

And I shattered right then and there, driving my body down into his mouth, pleading for him to fuck me.

He climbed back to his feet and bent me over the railing more to get just the right angle he needed.

"Oh trust me, Emilia, I'll fuck you. By the time I am done with you, the whole house is going to know I fucked you."*

He gave me no warning before his cock was buried to the hilt inside me, and I screamed out in pure euphoria. He pumped into me from behind as one hand reached around and grabbed me by my throat, bringing our bodies closer together. His other hand rested on my hips, where he used the position to thrust inside me harder. His fingers reached down

---

* Continue playing Sacrifice (feat. Jessie Reyez) - Black Atlass, Jessie Reyez

to swipe through my wet center before he forced them between my lips, not only keeping my screams quiet, but with his fingers thrusting inside my mouth, he was filling me up every which way, and the feeling of being full was exhilarating,

The orgasm that hit me next came in full force like a tsunami. The railing made a screeching sound where I held it firmly in my grip. This orgasm rippled through me in waves, and I could feel my own heartbeat in my throat, alive and beating like it wanted to crawl its way out. This was a high. It was an adrenaline rush being with him.

He grabbed a fistful of my hair and reared my head back so I could gaze back at him.

"Make sure to smile for the camera, baby, when I make you come all over my cock," he said, pushing my face up towards my security camera before biting down on my neck forcefully, while simultaneously ripping the anal beads from my body. Right as I imploded, my mouth dropping in a silent gasp, he grunted into my ear and spilled himself into me.

After Matteo came, he gently guided my leg back down to the ground where I couldn't help but shake on quivering legs.

He leaned down and took my lips in a soft, lingering kiss before bending down and licking the blood from my neck.

"You will be the death of me, Emilia."

CHAPTER TWENTY-ONE

MATTEO

I GROWLED INTO THE CROOK OF EMILIA'S NECK, BREATHING her in. The scent of her blood, her arousal and the very smell of just her filled my nose, and I'm grounded to the spot, grounded to this moment with her. In my desperate need for her, I'd sought her out, wanting to tell her everything. I'd had no idea if she would even bother to open the door for me after I left her back at the shooting range, but she did, and the words poured out of me. A jumbled mess of words, but words all the same.

I'd laid it all out for her at her feet, told her that she turned the volume down on the voices in my head. That in itself was a scary thought, not so much the demons in my head whispering to me daily that I was unworthy, but that this woman was the antidote, my reprieve.

I expected her to yell at me for how I left her, for my disobedience, for not doing the job I was hired to do, but she didn't do any of those things. Instead, she had pulled me into her room and thrown my own words back at me. Her giving me permission to use her in whatever way I saw fit to quiet the noise was all the confirmation I needed to ruin her to my heart's content. In every way I had been fantasizing about for weeks.

She'd looked up at me with such trust in those pools of cerulean sky eyes that I had felt my heart stop momentarily at the sight.

After that, it was like a switch had gone off in my head, and the beast I held on a leash escaped its restraints. I wanted Emilia in every way imaginable. She was like a drug, and I wanted to use her over and over again. Watching her crawl to me, degrading her and praising her, taking her in ways I had dreamed about had proven that my fantasies were nothing compared to the real thing. She was an enchantress, tempting my self-control. I may have been the one making the demands, but the way she moved her body was sinful; she knew she was the one in control of me.

As I carried her over to her shower to clean us off, I was mentally elsewhere. I was replaying those moments where I'd had her squirming underneath me as I teased her with her toy, the look on her face when I'd made her come. Hearing her scream my name was an adrenaline rush, a motivator to me to make her scream it more, until she was praying to me, like I was her new religion. And the way she sucked me off, I'd never been so hard in my life. I'd had Emilia's lips around my cock once before, but fuck, tonight felt different.

She'd worshiped my cock, worshiped me as she let me fuck her mouth. The second I saw her tears glide down her face like diamonds and saw the drool dripping from her mouth, my orgasm barreled up my spine and I was shooting my load right down her throat, totally enthralled. Enraptured by the woman underneath me, I had pulled her to me, wanting the world to know I was the one who smeared her makeup, that I was the one to make her break apart over and over again, and I knew she would get off if she felt that we could get caught. Which had led me to bring her outside to her balcony, so I could devour her.

I didn't need to hear her whimpers of pleasure to know she was turned on, her pussy drenching my face told me everything I needed to know. The thought of knowing her bodyguards could look up and get the perfect view of her spread pussy made her gush like a waterfall, and I loved being on the receiving end.

I also found out tonight that my little devil liked every one of her holes filled, and boy did I tuck that little information away for a rainy day.

Emilia had one of those walk-in stone showers with no door, and without missing a beat, she turned the nozzle on and water rained down on us from above. It was so hot, steam had already begun to fill the room.

Emilia stared at me with a lazy smile on her face, her hair drenched and her mascara smudged, and I was captivated. I felt the urge to kiss her, so I pushed her back into the wall and did just that. Her hands pulled at my hair as she deepened our kiss, grinding her body on me, looking for friction. My dick was already hard for her again, and with one quick sleight of my hand, I pushed inside her.

Her mouth stretched wide at the intrusion, and I watched as her eyes rolled briefly to the back of her head, before she swirled her hips in time with my languid thrusts. I'd fucked her before, but right now, I wanted to slow things down with her. I wanted to be in the moment, to enjoy the feel of her tight cunt throbbing around my cock, feeling how wet I made her as she slid up and down on me. Her pussy tightened its hold on me, to the point where I struggled to pull out to thrust back inside. She was so warm, so tight, and I wanted to bury myself in her every day if she'd allow me.

"Fuck, Emilia, your sweet little cunt is squeezing my cock so hard," I tell her.

"Oh my God! Don't … don't stop, Matteo," she panted in a breathless moan.

"Do you want to come again?"

She could barely get the word out of her mouth, but she faintly murmured her answer.

"Don't ever call me by my last name again, hmm," I demanded of her, thrusting just a bit harder now. "Only Matteo. Know that every time you call me by my first name, I'm replaying all the times you screamed it for me when you came."

I felt her pussy tighten at my words, at the meaning behind them.

She didn't answer me, lost in a trance, but I heard the mumblings of a response.

"You should know by now, I need your words." I grabbed her face so I could look into her eyes so she knew I was serious. I didn't ever want her calling me Mr. Ricci ever again, not after I have heard her moan and whimper and scream my name.

"Only Matteo," she panted.

"Good girl."

I felt her clench around me one more time, and I stared at her as she let go. She didn't close her eyes this time; she stared right back at me through her climax, letting me witness every emotion. Witnessing that vulnerability on her face, I released inside her. I came so hard, I saw star points behind my eyes and I could've collapsed right there and then. I drove myself inside her, loving the feeling of her filled and dripping with my come. I pulled out of her and slowly brought her legs back down. As soon as both feet were firmly down on the floor, I took my two fingers and pushed in between her legs, feeling my come inside her. I caught my come dripping down her lips and pushed it back inside her, wanting her absolutely filled with me.

Her gasp filled the room and it was like a symphony to my ears. I turned her around and reached for her shampoo. Squeezing the contents into my hand, I started to massage the product into Emilia's scalp with my hands. She moaned in delight as I dug in, leaning her head back so I could get more access.

We continued in silence as I washed the shampoo out of her hair and did the same thing with the conditioner. Being with her like this was strikingly intimate.

"You're good at this," she said, a touch of envy laced in her tone.

A smile formed, knowing that Emilia believed I did this with all women, and whether or not she wanted to admit it out loud, she was jealous of that insinuation.

"I am," I told her. "When my mom was diagnosed with cancer, she lost her ability to do simple tasks such as washing her hair. All we had was each other growing up; my father was out of the picture for as long as I could remember, and I was her caretaker most days. I hired an at-home nurse to help when I couldn't be there, but most days it was me taking care of her."

She spun in my arms, piercing me with her beautiful blue eyes. They weren't filled with pity, but with empathy, as she soaked my words in.

"I'm so sorry, Matteo, I had no idea."

"No need to apologize. How could you know? I don't go sleeping around with women and then take care of them by washing their hair."

"You did for me though," she replied.

I nodded in response to her statement. "Yes, I did for you." I leaned in and kissed her forehead. I turned off the shower head and grabbed the closest towel, bundling her up inside.

"Come on, *principessa*, let's get some sleep."

CHAPTER TWENTY-TWO

EMILIA

FOR THE NEXT TWO WEEKS, I WOKE UP TO MATTEO'S TONGUE buried between my legs. I was in the middle of a steamy dream starring him, when I felt rough hands part my thighs. I turned my head into my pillow and groaned, not wanting to wake Matteo up with my sex dreams. But then I felt his wet tongue glide through my slit from bottom to top, and suddenly I was wide awake, staring down at a lump under the sheets positioned right between my legs.

His assault on my clit had me gripping the sheets with my fists as I ground back into his face relentlessly, feeling the friction burn from his beard on my skin. I pressed myself deeper into him, circling my hips, showing him exactly where I needed him.

He sucked my clit into his mouth, making me cry out and arch my back when a knock sounded at the door. I froze in horror, but the knocking didn't phase Matteo in the slightest. He continued without missing a beat.

"Emilia, you up?" Dante's voice came from the other side. Luckily, Matteo was smart enough to have locked the door when he came in last night, because I'm not sure how I would have explained the bodyguard that was currently giving me head.

"Uh … yeah," I called out apprehensively. "Be out in five."

Matteo's head popped up from under the sheets, his lips glistening with me. He locked eyes with mine and licked his lips wickedly. "You won't need five minutes, I'll have you screaming my name in just under one," he said, pushing two fingers inside me.

"I … I'll meet you downstairs Dante," I yelled between my muffled moans.

"Sure thing," he replied before the sounds of his retreating footsteps filled the hallway.

My attention fell back to the incredibly sexy and talented man between my legs, and I closed my eyes, reveling in the way Matteo brought the most vile and explicit words from my mouth as he ravished me. And just like he promised me, I came into his mouth within forty seconds. He made sure to make me aware of that fact.

He kissed me before climbing out of my bed, and I stared after him as he walked naked into my bathroom. I sensed the grin on my face as I laid there post-orgasm, feeling like I could take on whatever today decided to throw at me.

I shoved my sheets back and rolled out of bed, throwing on my bathrobe as I crossed the room to my closet. I tossed on a black cropped tee and black leather pants before finding my favorite combat boots. Matteo exited the bathroom right as I finished up my makeup.

"Hi," he said from behind me.

"Hi," I responded, locking eyes with him in the mirror.

"I need to check in with my guys and see how things are doing over there. I'll catch up with you later tonight, yeah?"

He leaned down, kissing my neck, and I hummed in response to his touch.

"Mmm, I'll see you tonight."

He gave me one last look over his shoulder before opening up my door.

"I can't wait to find out what else makes you scream tonight."

And with a smirk, he was gone. And I was left reeling with the feeling that this could be us daily if we were a normal couple, and that crippled me where I stood.

I spent the day in and out of meetings with Dante and checking in on my businesses throughout the city. I end up at my club, *Envy*, the venue packed with party-goers dressed to impress. Girls and guys were scattered either at the bar or grinding on one another on the dance floor. A slight commotion catches my attention as I glance over at the VIP section, where I find a group of finance guys hitting on a bachelorette party. It's then that my eyes find one of the guys slipping something into a girl's drink while she's distracted, and I see red.

Without thinking or wasting another minute, I stormed over to the group, launching myself at the rapist and pinning him against the wall. His group of friends stood up as if to aid him, until one lethal look from me had them dispersing. The girls looked on in shock.

"Don't drink any of that. My security guards will escort you back to a new VIP room with fresh drinks made by the bartender, on me," I told them. They nod in appreciation before following my guards down the hall. I turn my head to look at the pathetic boy in front of me.

"So, you like to drug your victims?" I asked, choking him more with my forearm. "Well you're about to find out first-hand how I like to play with *my* victims."

I dragged him into the club basement where I had some of my men tie him to a chair.

"You think it's okay to drug a woman?"

He didn't answer, his face still remaining stoic, until he saw me grab a tire iron from my weapons cabinet. He started to squirm in his chair, and it was not long before I saw a dark spot on his pants.

I gripped the bat in my hands and brought it barreling down full force onto one of his legs. I heard the bone crunch right before he screamed in agony. Tears spilled from his eyes, but I was numb to it all.

"Answer me! You think it's okay to drug a woman? To take away her right to say no?"

He sobbed into his chest as he replied with a screaming no.

I was driving the bat back down onto his already shattered leg when Dante came rushing into my office.

"It's happening tonight," he informed me.

He looked over the scene in front of him, his mouth twitching in amusement.

"Just couldn't help yourself, could you?" He laughed, motioning for me to follow him out of the room.

"Take care of this," I commanded my guards.

"You're a hundred percent on this, Dante? Our men at the docks confirmed it's her shipment?" I asked as we make our way into my office.

We couldn't afford to be wrong, to make an assumption. I'd put my reputation on the line and my ego aside to work closely with the Vitales, another mafia family running in Chicago, in order to cross briefly into their turf, in the hopes of catching Camila.

Deep down I knew she wouldn't be there herself; she never did any of the heavy lifting. Just sat back on her throne and let her drug lords move her merchandise. That wasn't to say Camila wasn't lethal—she certainly had blood on her hands. When I was first sold into her business, I became envious of her. Not because of the business she dealt in, but rather because of the power she held over her men. That she was in control over her own fate, unlike me. I vowed to myself that when I escaped, I'd be a woman like her. Powerful enough that no man could ever do to me what they had already done.

Tonight my intention was to send her a message.

"The Fisherman confirmed not too long ago it was her cargo ship. They should be docking in twenty minutes."

Standing up from my desk, I pulled my gun from my back and released the magazine, making sure I had a full mag before reinserting it and racking a bullet into the chamber.

"Tell the boys to suit up. No one is leaving those docks unless they're in a body bag."

I rounded the desk, stalking past Dante, ready for war.

*We arrived at the docks with five minutes to spare. As soon as *La Corredora's* men left that cargo ship and unloaded their shipment into the onsite warehouse, my men and I would be ready to go on the offense.

---

*   Born Ready - Zayde Wolf

I threw on my kevlar vest, complete with a slot for my guns and pockets for extra magazines and my knife. Strapped to my back, I had my scabbard with my katana sword inside, and secured to both thighs, I had my daggers.

"Everyone ready and in position?" I asked, looking over to Dante to see him strapping his thigh holster into place.

He tapped his ear piece, rattling off commands and listening intently before nodding back over to me.

"We're all good on our end. ETA 1 minute."

I nodded in response before preparing myself for what was to come. Camila had taken everything from me, and now I was going to hit her back where it would hurt her the most. She was encroaching on my city, and I wasn't going to have that. She would not become powerful here, not when I ran this city.

My men held their positions behind me as I watched her men dock their ship at the port. I counted twelve men to my six, but I didn't feel the odds stacked against us. Instead, I felt bloodlust fuel me. I felt years of built-up anger and defiance come bubbling to the surface, and I was itching to enact my revenge.

My body tensed, and I couldn't help my emotions as they took over. My eyes pricked with unshed tears, and my finger-nails punctured the skin of my palms as I watched thirty scared and malnourished women exit a shipping container in nothing but their undergarments. Bile rose to my mouth, but I fought the urge to be sick. Flashbacks filtered through my head as I watched the men leer and poke at them in crude ways, herding them into the warehouse. I swallowed the painful lump in my throat and, with fire coursing through my veins and vengeance on my mind, I called the command that would lead my men and I into battle.*

I led the charge, my men flanking me three to a side as we

---

* Stop playing Born Ready - Zayde Wolf

crossed the empty lot towards the warehouse. I'd planned this attack in my head for years, and tonight it would finally come to fruition. I signaled three of my men to come in from the back, trapping them from both sides, while Dante and two of my other men, Stefan and Lorenzo, entered through the front door.

*As soon as I walked through the front, my hands were already pulling my guns from their holsters, and I pulled the trigger at any man within range with a gun. My third shot ripped through a man's chest, but I didn't wait for the body to hit the ground. I knew he was dead from the moment my bullet left the chamber. Shots echoed inside the steel building, and I smelled the sulfur and blood in the air, as Camila's men came to meet mine in bloodshed.

A man rounded the corner, firing off a shot at my head, but his aim was off and hit the wood pallet behind me. His next shot was more on point, but I sidestepped out of the way and fired a bullet back. I watched in rapture as the bullet sliced right through one side of his head before exiting through the other side. Normally, I would've stopped and enjoyed my work, but Camila's lower informants were not a priority to me.

I heard shouting in all directions in both English and Spanish, but I didn't dare stop. I could only pray that I didn't lose another one of my men tonight. I had my target.

"Kill the lower men, but the lieutenants we leave injured," I called out to my men within earshot.

After five long minutes of endless screaming and the sharp, high-pitched sounds of bullets firing from their weapons, the warehouse was ghostly silent. I prayed to God, and knew he must have listened when I heard all six of my men radio in that they were all accounted for. I was about to radio in my position when my target slunk from his hiding

---

* Monster - Ruelle

spot and rounded the corner. I fired off a bullet right through the back of his leg, directly into his kneecap. He went down hard, but he managed to hold onto his weapon.

He screamed in agony as he twisted his body, his gun lifted and directly at me. I didn't even flinch as I stared at the barrel of a gun. I dove for the ground as we both discharged our weapons. His shot would've hit its mark in my chest if I hadn't moved. Instead, it grazed my arm. and the bite strung, but my adrenaline was flowing and I ignored it for now. I heard the clatter of his gun on the concrete as he grabbed for his hand where he now only had three fingers.

I squatted down next to him and dug the nozzle of my gun into his wound at his knee, and he squirmed in anguish, spit flying from his mouth as he bit down on his pain.

"Hello, Andreas, did you miss me?" I taunted.

"Fuck you, puta," he spat at me. I didn't recoil as I wiped his saliva from my face with my sleeve. Instead, I pushed harder into the gaping hole at his knee until profanities were pouring from his mouth.

I radioed in to Dante.

"Fan out to the perimeter. I need ten minutes alone with our friend here. Get Enzo to round up the girls."

"On it," he replied, and then I went radio silent.

"Tell me, Andreas, have you ever heard of the game Operation?" I stared down at him, a gleam of malicious intent in my eyes. I smiled cruelly, a satisfied sense of cold amusement falling over me as I turned off my humanity for the next ten minutes.

"Now, let's have some fun," I said tauntingly, as I took my dagger and got to work.

CHAPTER TWENTY-THREE

EMILIA

*I DUG MY DAGGER DEEP INTO THE BULLET WOUND IN HIS KNEE and started to carve upward. All the while, he screamed, and it was like a beautiful harmony to my ears.

"Tell me where Camila is," I ordered him.

He bit down hard on his lips, refusing to give me anything, so I changed up tactics. I moved my attention back toward his hand, where he now only had his three fingers left.

"What a shame to lose your trigger finger, Andreas," I said with disdain. "I know how much you loved to use that when you couldn't get your way. I hope you're ambidextrous, for your sake. We both know how much Camila loathes deadweight."

He reared his head and spat in my direction.

"I remember you, *puta*. I miss your fiery attitude and boy did I love to shut you up and punish you for it," he began to say, but he cut himself off with a scream as I sawed off his middle finger.

"Yeah, I remember you too, *cabron*. I remember everything from those days, and I certainly remember everything you did

---

*   Fed Up - Ghostemane

to me. So, consider this my vengeance. Except the difference between you and me, Andreas, is that I finish the job."

I leaned down and whispered calmly in his ear, "You should have killed me when you had the chance, because now it's my turn to play."

Inside my blood boils at this man underneath me. The Emilia ten years ago would have been petrified by the man before her. Every time she saw his face, she knew to expect the worst from him, so her coping mechanism was to block it all out. But the powerful woman I am today can't block those things that were done to her. That scared girl needed a woman like me to fight for her. She had only escaped by pure luck and will, and I'm proud of her for that. She'd left behind bodies for Camila to clean up, but I, on the other hand, wouldn't be running from Camila. I was taking the fight to her.

"Do your worst, I won't tell you anything," he seethed at me, his tone firm, but for a split second I could see a flicker of fear in his eyes.

"You'll regret those words, Andreas. There are worse things than death," I informed him before letting the dark demon inside me out of its cage.

I started to slice away at skin, peeling back layers, listening to the man I hated more than my ex-husband scream his lungs out.

"Scream all you want, no one is coming to save you," I sneered. "Weren't those the words you told me when you forced yourself on me repeatedly?"

I pierced his abdomen and began to hack away, cutting through skin and muscle. Out of the corner of my eye, I saw him start to fade at the pain.

I cocked my hand back and slapped him across the face, jostling him awake, adrenaline likely flooding his veins in fight-or-flight response.

"Can't have you falling asleep and missing the best part, Andreas," I taunted.

With his eyes full of hatred, he watched me as I buried my hand inside his body and ripped out his spleen. His eyes blew wide with terror and shock, and I stared down in unparalleled pleasure.

"They say you can live without your spleen, but those without it are prone to infections and have a higher risk of bleeding," I informed him. "Now, I'm no doctor, but judging by your injuries, you may very well bleed out."

"Fuck you!"

"Hmm, what should I take next? Your kidneys? I heard you can live without one of those too," I told him as I started to slice back into him. "But I need you to give *her* a message for me."

"And ... what's that?" A wet, gurgling sound coming from the back of his throat.

I lowered my body until I could feel his labored breaths on my face.

"Any of her men that puts one toe inside my city will end up dead."

"You'll start a war ..." he wheezed. "She'll come for you."

I stood up to my full height and peered down at the cockroach below me.

"Let her. I'll be waiting."*

And with those parting words to one of the ghosts that has haunted me for well over a decade, I pulled the katana sword from its sheath and brought it down full force at his neck, beheading him.

---

* Stop playing Fed Up - Ghostemane

I squared my shoulders and rolled out my neck, trying to clear up the kinks. After hacking off Andreas' head, I had used my sword to chisel away at his other body parts, rearranging them to look like a jigsaw puzzle. I knew the FBI would find him, and once they knew who he was and who he worked for, the media would catch wind of it, and photos from the crime scene would be leaked to the world. And then Camila would know I was coming for her when one of her most prized drug lords was featured on the news with his head gone and his middle finger flipping her off.

I closed my eyes and reined in the darkness, remembering who I was, who I needed to be now in this moment. In … one, two, three. Out … one, two, three. The underworld talked, and within a year they had deemed me *Serpent Queen*, not only for the tattoo coiled around my neck, but because some snakes decapitate their prey before swallowing them whole. Tonight, I'd let that side of me come out. The side I keep buried at all costs, unless absolutely necessary. But now I needed to be Emilia DeLuca, businesswoman to the citizens of Chicago.

I cleared my head and radioed in to Dante.

"He wouldn't give her up, but the message I left for her should draw her in," I debriefed him.

He responded, informing me that the girls were on the bus and en route, and that in three minutes authorities would be flooding the docks.

I wiped the blood from my sword on his clothes before putting it away and making my way toward the exit. There was not much I could do about the blood that now painted my face and hands like a second layer of skin, so I didn't bother trying to clean myself up.

*I exited the warehouse on high alert, hearing the sirens in the distance, knowing they were getting closer.

I cross the parking lot, my hand hovering over the door when I see Matteo's reflection in the driver's side window, and the gun he has leveled at the back of my head.

"So the rumors are true then?" Disgust coated the words that came to me from the dark.

I lifted my hands in the air in surrender and turned slowly toward him, my eyes narrowing at the muzzle of the gun inches from my forehead.

"And what rumors would those be, Mr. Ricci?" I countered, purposefully choosing not to use his first name, knowing it would irritate him. And I knew it had when I saw the slight twitch under his right eye, giving him away.

He took in my appearance briefly, from the dark red that stained my hands to the ichor from Andreas that now stained my clothes.

"That you're a monster," he accused me. I didn't let it show on my face, but his venomous words hit their mark and seeped into my skin like poison.

"In order to fight the monsters at your doorstep, you have to become an even worse one yourself," I replied. "And monsters thrive better in the dark."

"This isn't you," he said, shaking his head, as if he was trying to piece together all the facts.

"You're wrong. This is who I am. I am a monster; you just choose not to believe it. But I guarantee you, whatever you think you know is not the whole truth."

The sirens' wail is closer now, and I can see the red-and-blue lights barreling down the road in the distance.

---

* Eyes Don't Lie - Dark Mage, JB RICKY, EYLA

"Then what is the truth?" Matteo demanded, not phased by the incoming lights.

"Get in the car and I'll show you, but we have to go now."

"Why should I trust you?"

"You can't trust me. But I know you, and deep down you want to know the truth more than you want to turn me over to the authorities."

He didn't reply, but I could see that my words were getting to him.

"Last chance, Matteo. What's it going to be?"

CHAPTER TWENTY-FOUR

MATTEO

"LAST CHANCE, MATTEO. WHAT'S IT GOING TO BE?" EMILIA demanded from me. I stared over at her in disbelief, praying that what Tobias and I had seen from a distance was out of context and that I had it all wrong. I knew from working with her that she did conduct business illegally, but she was good at hiding her tracks from the authorities. But this was human trafficking. That didn't seem like Emilia's style.

I glanced back down at her, wondering whose blood marred her skin. Was it hers or someone else's? Emilia looked as if she had just stepped off the set of a horror movie, but this wasn't Hollywood, and that wasn't fake blood on her skin.

I could hear the sirens approaching and knew I had to make a decision. She had me figured out, and that was scary. I did want to know the truth more than I wanted to see hand-cuffs on her.

"Get in the car," I instructed her, finally voicing an answer, lowering my weapon and moving toward her passenger door.

She nodded in reply and followed my directions. The second she turned the car on, she put it in drive and slammed on the gas, whipping the car in the opposite direction from the oncoming lights.

I kept my weapon trained on her as she maneuvered through the streets of Chicago, avoiding the red-and-blue lights that chased us. Within minutes, she parked the car inside a mechanic shop and hopped out. I followed her, my gun still aimed at her as she quickly shut the bay door, hiding us from the agents flooding the streets.

"What are you doing, Emilia?"

She faced me head on and walked straight at me, no fear in her eyes as she stared down the barrel of my gun.

"Avoiding the feds, Matteo. You want the truth, I'm going to give it to you."

She hooks her thumb to her left, and I snuck a glance in that direction, my eyes focused on the blacked-out Dodge Challenger.

"We needed a new ride first," she simply stated, before turning her back on me and heading for the vehicle.

I watched her, awestruck, as she bent over the driver's side seat and yanked down the compartment under the steering wheel.

"Is hot-wiring a vehicle also on your list of hidden talents?"

Despite the situation, I couldn't help the question that fell from my mouth, my eyes drifting down to her ass and how nicely it stretched out those pants.

"It's definitely one of them," she agreed, satisfied with her work when she heard the engine turn over. "Get in the car," she said, looking over at me as she bent down to open up the other bay door. I hesitated, wary of her movements. She dared to laugh.

"I'm not going to run, Matteo."

I walked to the passenger side, but still watched every move she made until she was sitting in the vehicle next to me.

Emilia revved the engine and flew out of the garage, turning north. We drove for another twenty minutes or so, until Emilia started to slow down the car to drive through residential areas. It's when she parked the car on the side of the road that I became agitated.

"Is this a joke, Emilia? What are we doing in North Center?"

Despite her chaotic appearance, Emilia sat there breathing calmly, yet the fidgeting of her hands made me think she was nervous.

*"This isn't a joke, Matteo. Not this. Not them."

"Who's them?"

She looked out her window at the white single-family home with the brick exterior. I look past her at the house she was gazing at lovingly. There was a kid's bike tossed lazily in the front yard, a beautiful garden that bordered the front steps, and right there on the front porch were two pastel colored rocking chairs that faced the street.

My gaze swung over to the bay window to the right, and together we watched as a woman cradled her daughter to her chest, soothing her back to sleep. She looked to be in her late twenties, give or take, with long blonde hair. I was too far to see any other intimate details about this woman, but I could tell she was beautiful. A man came up behind her and hugged her, burying his face in the crook in her neck, and her laugh felt contagious, as the touch filled her with emotion.

"Her name is Eliza Bronwyn. Age 33. Married to Nathan Bronwyn. They had a small wedding in his parent's backyard out in Holland, Michigan, about fifty guests or so. They have a daughter named Isabel, but she likes to go by Izzy. She's four years old and looks just like her mom," Emilia rattled off to me.

"Eliza has her own private practice catering to young children and women, helping them get back on their feet after tragedy, and her husband Nathan is CFO of a small bank. They met almost to this day, six years ago. Quite literally ran

---

* Monsters - Tommee Profit, XEAH | Spotify Playlist

into each other. She was cramming for a last study session over at Grant Park when he literally fell on her because he was on a business call." She smiled at the memory as if she were there. "He immediately hung up his call and began to apologize profusely. They ended up talking for two hours, and when she started to leave, he asked her out on a date, and now … now they live here," she finished, a lone tear forming in her eyes.

She blinked hard, twice, the tear disappearing.

I cleared my throat, dissecting all the information she just threw my way.

"How do you know Eliza Bronwyn? What is the connection between her and you and what I saw happen tonight?"

She swiveled in her seat, her brows furrowed, and I saw her tense facial expression and wide eyes.

"Eliza was one of the girls that was trafficked by *La Corredora*," she started, but what she said next had me rooted to the spot. "… And she was also my cellmate."

Those words had me in a chokehold. Emilia might as well have driven her dagger through my torso and pinned me to the seat, because that's honestly how I felt in this moment.

"My husband, Romeo, got bored of me when I couldn't deliver him an heir, so when he saw an opportunity to get rid of me and shack up with his mistress, he took it. He sold me to Camila when I was just shy of nineteen. He had me drugged and when I woke up, I was laying in a 10x10 concrete cell on a soiled mattress that reeked of urine. Eliza was there. She was the one that had to break the news of my fate for the next four years."

She paused, taking in deep breaths, and I got lost in her, completely enraptured by her resilience and everything she must have endured at such a young age.

"They kept us locked up like animals in a zoo. When the door would open to our cell, we never knew if we would come back."

"The first time they pulled me from my cot, I was asleep

and I fought like hell. Kicking, biting, screaming until I was hoarse. I learned quickly how they would shut up the women who rebelled," she disclosed, lifting her shirt to reveal a pink raised scar on the side of her body. I don't know how I missed it before.

"They used a cattle prod on us when we would act out," she quietly whispered. "The men would clean us up in the communal showers before delivering us to the men who had paid for our services, but not before they had some fun at our expense. The men they handed us off to weren't any better. Camila's men would tie us to the bed so we couldn't run, and the men did whatever they wanted to us in that allotted time." Tears trickled down her face like shooting stars as she was forced back into the memory.

"Sometimes they would bring friends and take turns with us."

Her hands came up to wrap themselves around her body, and I saw red. I was enraged hearing what was done to Emilia and these women, and my vision went hazy. It was like someone had thrown a curtain over my eyes and it was bright fucking red. If Emilia hadn't already killed her ex-husband, I would've tracked him down and done a lot worse. But *La Corredora*, she was the leader of this human trafficking ring, and she was still out there.

Finally, after I got my breathing to stabilize, I reached out to touch her knee, but she flinched, still lost in her past. I retracted my hand, not wanting to spook her.

"How did you escape?"

She pinned me with her stare, an unsettling glaze coating her eyes as she forced herself deeper into the memory.

"The guards got sloppy," she started to say, shifting the gear back into drive and pulling back onto the street. She drove south, back toward Navy Pier. We drove in silence for a bit, and I sat there patiently waiting, not wanting to rush her story. I no longer aimed the gun at her, but it did rest in my lap, God forbid I needed it.

"There was a time we thought we were going to be rescued by the police," Emilia piped up from her seat. My eyes drifted back toward her, wanting to hang onto every last word.

"We had overheard Camila's men whispering in the halls about a raid not too far from where we were being kept."

We're stopped at a streetlight, and the glow from the light casts Emilia in a red tint, making the blood painted on her skin stand out.

"Camila's men were spread thin as it was with the authorities getting too close, and there were less men to watch over us. With the feds in Camila's backyard, her men were frantic, and they started to make small mistakes here and there."

Emilia sits there, drenched in the green light now, and I can't help but think that green is more suited to her.

"One night they forgot to lock the door to our cell, and I grabbed Eliza and dashed for a sliver of hope, a chance of freedom. There was a good chance my spontaneous breakout would be futile, but I was willing to risk death. At least in death I would have been free, and this death would have been honorable. I knew that if I died in that prison, it would be because I'd fought to escape it," she disclosed with a sad grimace.

"There were only two guards stationed at the end of the hall, and with nothing left to lose, I ran like hell for them, taking one out at the back of their knee. I used the skills that my father had drilled into me and was able to grab the guard's gun. With a bullet at close range to the base of his spine, I knew he wouldn't be following us. The other guard tried to shoot at me, but I used his paralyzed friend as a shield and shot him twice in the chest.

"From there, Eliza and I ran for the red door that had always haunted our nightmares, knowing that on the other side was freedom."

She stopped again at the side of the street. This time we were in a neighborhood just outside Lincoln Park.

"My one regret that night was not being able to save the rest of those girls. After I had gotten Eliza and me to safety, I tracked down Dante, and he came for us and got us out. It was upon reuniting with him that I learned of my father's fate.

"Everything that had once belonged to my father was now in my ex-husband's possession. I made sure my first appearance back into reality was to pay him a visit, and well, you already know that story. Once I was able to regain my father's earnings, I gave Eliza money to start a new life wherever she wanted. We stayed in touch over the years, and I send the women I saved to her to save them in other ways."

I went to open my mouth to commend her for her valor and tenderness when Emilia spoke up again.

"This is Hailey Martinez," she informed me, pointing up at the ranch-style home stretched out before me. It was a beautiful yet simple home, and through the window I could faintly make out a woman in her early twenties sprawled out on the living room couch reading.

"Hailey was kidnapped when she was seventeen years old from the mall. She turns twenty-one next week. I saved her from Camila two years ago and helped her reunite with her family, who never gave up searching for their little girl. It took a lot of therapy and acceptance, but she eventually graduated from high school and is now enrolled in the University of Chicago in the writing program. She wants to be an author someday.

"These are just two of the hundreds of women I save from the clutches of Camila. Unfortunately, I cannot save them all, and it's those women who haunt me. Even the ones I have freed, I can't save them all completely in the end."

"How do you fund a new life for them all?" I asked quietly.

"You're a smart man, Matteo, I'm sure you can figure it out."

"All of your illegal dealings."

She laughed at my statement. "Not all of my dealings are illegal, you know. All of my businesses are legitimate. What I do on the side, though, that's different. That funds this whole operation."

"That's a noble thing, despite where the money comes from."

"I'm the monster they need to fight for them. I'm the monster lurking in the shadows ready to slaughter their demons, and I will happily carry that burden if it means these women have a chance at happiness again."

Her eyes were like shooting daggers as they pinned me in my seat.

"So yes, Matteo, I may be a monster, but I'm *their* monster."

CHAPTER TWENTY-FIVE

EMILIA

*THE RIDE HOME WAS SILENT. WHAT ELSE WAS THERE TO SAY? Matteo Ricci now knew everything about me. All the skeletons I had buried in the back of the closet, all of my darkest memories, thrust out into the world for him to see and judge.

As I drove the familiar route back home, I thought back on everything I'd told Matteo. From murdering my ex-husband, to being sold into a human trafficking ring, I came to the realization that he hadn't actually judged me for either. Holding me at gunpoint earlier, I chalked that up to a misunderstanding and him not having the full picture. But that still didn't mean I trusted him.

Matteo didn't utter a word to me the entire drive back. Instead, he sat there mute, most likely sifting through all of the information I'd unloaded onto his lap.

Tonight I was able to send a message to Camila, and this time I hope she heard it loud and clear. I was not fucking around when it came to keeping my city protected from the likes of her and what she represented. If she wanted a war, she'd get one.

---

* No Time to Die - Billie Eilish

I'd planned my attack since my first day locked in that cage like an animal. But the beast that I kept locked up inside me had been created by her; and her creation would be her downfall.

The gates swung open upon my arrival, and the car wound its way around the bends leading up to the main drive. Before I'd left, I had sent a text to Dante, and through the windshield I watched as he stood fuming outside the doors, waiting. He had his arms crossed over his broad chest, and a permanent scowl on his face, all directed toward the man sitting next to me.

I started to make my way inside, craving nothing more than a hot shower to wash this blood off of me. I wasn't lying to Matteo when I said I would become this monster for them. But despite knowing I *had* to, it didn't mean I *wanted* to. In a way, I envied Matteo. He ran his own gun-for-hire business out in the open and never had to worry if someone was going to take a shot at him.

As I pass by Dante, I noticed three more of my body-guards standing just inside the door to my estate on high alert.

"I want him locked up and questioned," I demanded of Dante.

"Emilia—" Matteo spoke up behind me, but I ignored his pleas. I couldn't be emotional right now. I was already at my max today.

Dante turned his head toward me and dipped his chin in understanding as I walked past the rest of my men and up the stairs. They didn't even balk at the sight of me drenched in blood. I didn't turn back at Matteo's shouts of my name.

*Finally alone, I tore the clothes from my body and stared at myself in the mirror. I had a burn mark running perpendicular to my body, and there was blood that dripped from the wound now dried on my arm from the bullet that had grazed me earlier. But for the most part, besides a few bruises, my body remained unscathed. My gaze dropped lower, to the snake that wrapped itself around my body protectively, its head curling up under my chin. I let my mind wander when I first got that tattoo. It had been two months after I had escaped from that prison. When I'd told her what I wanted done, she looked at me not with pity, but in solidarity, and she'd taken her time perfecting my Medusa tattoo. My eyes glanced briefly at the black and gray artwork. Medusa's head was thrown back in a warrior cry, with snakes cascading down from the crown of her head, but one snake branched off from the rest and wrapped its way around my back and up my neck, a symbol of rebirth and transformation.

In the shower, I let the water wash away my sins as if I was being reborn. I stood there, allowing the scalding hot water to burn my skin, until it was red and raw. Frozen in place, I followed the path of the red-tinted water as it circled the drain. I wouldn't let Matteo's betrayal ruin a good night. We'd saved dozens of girls tonight, and that was something to be proud of. After showering, I walked into my room, not bothering with a towel, and made my way into my walk-in closet.

---

* Continue to play No Time to Die - Billie Eilish

Dressed in high-waisted black pants and a black crop top and small heels, I made my way downstairs. As I descended the stairs, I threw my wet hair up in a bun.

As I left, I notice Dante was absent and I knew at this moment he probably had Matteo tied up downstairs in the basement. I'd deal with that situation later. Right now I had more important things to take care of.

Twenty minutes later, I pulled up to an estate as big as my own. Hidden away in a town called Barrington, I'd purchased a second home. With 12,000 square feet, this place was a sanctuary for the women I rescued. It was a place they could feel safe, surrounded by other women who understood what they had been through. I had even hired women bodyguards, on-call doctors, and therapists should they need them. I bought this home in cash, making sure my real name wasn't on it and it couldn't be traced back to me.

The estate sat on five acres and was surrounded by woods. I'd chosen this place because it provided the women with unmatched privacy and a beautiful view of a serene creek nearby. Inside, you were greeted by a grand foyer and soaring ceilings with stunning European windows that let in natural light. Spread throughout the estate were twelve bedrooms large enough that two women could easily sleep in one and still be comfortable. On the main floor, the foyer opened up into a grand dining room with a beautiful oak table long enough to fit them all, and a welcoming family room that opened out into a sprawling terrace that overlooked the back-yard, which was equipped with a heated saltwater pool and a cute outdoor oasis to escape to. Upstairs, along with the bedrooms, was a beautiful library that reminded me a bit of the one from that Disney movie.

I'd bought this house with the intention of rescuing women from these trafficking rings and offering them a safe haven. A place where they could rest their heads at night and not feel the need to lock their doors in fear of someone coming to drag them from their beds for nefarious things. A refuge for them to get their bearings before they had to face reality again.

I made sure to help them find their path back to the world, whether that be rejoining their loved ones or providing them with a whole new identity. I got these women back on their feet, aided them in finding a job or enrolling them in school, and funded their new lives on one condition: they give therapy a try. While it may not have worked for me, I wanted to give these women a fighting chance at a better life, and that began with talking to someone.

I stared up at the gray brick exterior as I strode through the bright yellow door.* I was greeted by our cute and fluffy black German Shepherd, Bronco. I had him trained to be a therapy dog and to help comfort the women. He was a hit with the ladies around here and received all the love and attention he deserved.

"Hi sweet boy," I murmured to him, scratching just behind his ear like he loved. "Where are the ladies?"

He wagged his tail in response and started to make his way into the family room where a good amount of the girls sat on couches and on the floor. Some were huddled together, quietly talking amongst themselves, while others kept to themselves

---

* Stop playing No Time to Die - Billie Eilish

and sipped piping hot tea. I took these strong, resilient women in and held back the tears that wanted to escape.

"Hello, ladies," I started, drawing their immediate attention. I read the expressions on their faces. Some looked up at me in awe as if I were their guardian angel. Others looked at me with curiosity, and some glared at me with distrust. I didn't blame them. They'd gone from a prison to this, with no information.

"My name is Emilia," I told them, sitting down on a lounge chair closest to them.

"You are safe here, I promise. Men are not allowed on my estate and you are not prisoners. You are free to leave at any time. Although, I do encourage you to stay and heal and to give yourself time to stand back on your feet," I informed them, giving the same speech I gave every new woman that came through that door.

"Under my roof, you will be provided for. Food, clothing, books, education, and any medical needs."

A small, petite brunette in the back corner, the one whose glare would strike me down if I wasn't who I was, spoke up.

"Why are you doing all of this? What do you get out of it?" she spat out.

I smiled warmly over at her, my eyes going soft because I saw the fire raging inside her. She reminded me a lot of myself when I escaped. She was going to make it.

"Because I too was where you were. My husband sold me to Camila almost fifteen years ago. I was held prisoner just like all of you were. I suffered under the same conditions, fell prey to the same despicable actions they put you all through, and I have the scars to prove it. Ten years ago, I escaped and fought my way out and for a better life. I've been helping women escape since then, giving them a safe place to live until they feel like they're ready to start living again.

"We are not defined by what happened to us. The fact that

you are here today, alive, doesn't make you victims, but survivors. *Warriors.* You fought to live another day, and another one after that, and another after that. Despite being thrust into darkness, you are here thriving in spite of it. I'm giving you a second chance at life, so take it with both hands and choose to live."

I stayed for a little bit longer, getting to know these strong women before me. I took in the women sitting in front of me and committed their names and their stories to memory.

The one who spoke up earlier that reminded me of myself was Brianna Wilder, twenty-two years old, and was kidnapped outside her local mall in Seattle. The two girls who remained quiet but attentive to every word I've said were Charlotte and Luna, both twenty years old. Charlotte was sold to Camila by her mother in exchange for money to buy heroin, and Luna was taken from a college campus after she tried to walk home from a frat party.

The three girls who sat cross-legged on the couch were all in their early twenties as well. Aria, Lily, and Nora. In my eyes, they were still young girls who deserved a life filled with love, making mistakes and reveling in their young twenties. Instead, they'd faced their worst nightmare and were exposed to such traumatic experiences that no one should have had to go through. Camila took away their innocence and trust.

I took in each woman before me, admiring their bravery and praying that I could be a beacon of light in their lives. I hoped that in time, they'd learn to trust again, open up again to someone, and maybe have the courage to fall in love, in spite of the things they had endured.

As I sunk further into the sofa cushion, I briefly wondered if I would ever be able to attain that goal. My thoughts drifted back to Matteo and what awaited me back home.

My head and heart were at a ceasefire. My heart felt like it was splitting in two, but I was used to betrayal, so it shouldn't hurt as much as it did. But deep down in my subconscious, a part of myself that didn't want to admit it knew why this particular betrayal hurt, and that was not something I was willing or ready to face.

Instead, I forgot my problems for the night and instead I focused on being present with the women before me.

CHAPTER TWENTY-SIX

MATTEO

Blood dripped from my swollen mouth as Dante's fists met my flesh once more. More of my blood lay in pools by my feet from previous injuries inflicted by Emilia's men. Her men had dragged me down into the underbelly of her estate, into a non-disclosed room with cement floors and bare walls. From the ceiling hung two steel chains with shackles at the ends. I was surprised to find that this isolated room was clean. There was no dried blood coating the dull, gray floor like I had expected. But then again, I couldn't picture Emilia bringing an enemy into the sanctuary of her estate. She was definitely smarter than that. I must be the exception.

Despite being strapped to this chair, an enemy before them, I didn't blame her men for following their orders. Hell, I didn't even blame Emilia for making the call.

If I were in her position, I would have done exactly the same thing. If one of my men had underestimated me and held me at gunpoint, I probably would have done a lot worse.

My mind disassociated from my body and the fists raining down on me, and I drifted off to thoughts of Emilia. It had been hours since she had left me at the hands of her men, and I wondered where she had gone off to. I knew she hadn't stayed here long. I only knew this because I felt the loss of her presence. Call me crazy, but I could sense if she was nearby. It's like the hairs on my neck stood at attention when she was close, and I had felt nothing for the last five hours.

After parting ways with her that morning, I had met with Tobias for a check-in. While I was deep inside Emilia's rank, Tobias was my liaison between me and the FBI. It was through Tobias that I had discovered that Camila had a shipment entering the docks later this evening, docks that were controlled by the Fisherman.

Emilia was planning something big and had been for weeks, and I'd been none the wiser.

Every one of Emilia's men had been so preoccupied that day, easily distracted, including Emilia herself, that no one had noticed I wasn't there. I'd followed her from a distance that day, both enraptured and curious as to her plan.

Later that evening, Tobias was in position on a nearby roof, his sniper rifle aimed at the chaos that was soon to unfold below us. While Tobias kept guard from an aerial perspective, I crept along the shadows of buildings, drawing closer to the action. From my vantage point, I could see Emilia strapping on tactical gear. Her raven-colored hair was tied back, the ends of it skimming her lower back, but poking through her curtain of hair was a beautiful katana sword. Even from this distance, I could tell the pommel was intricate and stunning.

As my eyes trailed lower down her body, I saw the guns

and knives strapped to her thighs. She reminded me of a modern-day Athena, a goddess warrior ready for battle, and I stood there, mouth open, absolutely awestruck by this woman. I stood there watching as Emilia led her charge into the building, and when the gunshots started firing, before I could even blink I was racing toward the battle.

I could hear Tobias firing off profanities in my ear. I knew I was deviating from what we'd come here to do, but my feet had a mind of their own. I raced inside the building, staying low and out of sight. Loud screams and gunfire fell upon my ears, and I fought against my instinct to jump into the fray, as I normally would have done.

This was a battlefield, more or less. It may not have been in a country far across the ocean in a desert, but this was still a war zone. Emilia's war was inevitable, whether it was here or overseas.

I peered around the corner to find Stefan in a face-off with one of Camila's men. The man didn't even see it coming; Stefan was quick to the trigger and fired before the man could even move a muscle. The man's brains and blood splattered behind him as the bullet tore through his head. Stefan was already moving before the body had hit the floor, but with the sounds of gunfire echoing loudly in this steel trap, he didn't see the second man sneak up from behind him. Before he could turn fully to assess the threat, I came out from my hiding spot and fired my gun at Camila's man who had his gun aimed at Stefan's head.

One shot rang out, hitting him in his chest. Stefan turned at the sound and raised his weapon, but my second shot had already fired and landed directly in the man's throat. His body sank to the floor, the man's weapon falling from his hand, as he brought his hand to his throat as if to stop the blood from pouring out. It wouldn't stop, though. He would bleed out slowly and painfully. The man was still on his knees, clawing at his throat, his eyes wide in panic at the thought of death. I raised my arm once more, the nozzle of my gun pressed to the man's forehead, and pulled the trigger. The man's body went limp and collapsed backward onto the floor.

I felt a hand squeeze my shoulder. I turned my head to find Stefan looking at me with both shock and gratitude. He gave me a nod of respect, but before I could do anything in return he was already running off.

I slunk back into the shadows once more. Although I had saved Stefan's life, he knew I wasn't supposed to be here. I was supposed to be a ghost, but instead I showed my hand and I had a feeling it would bite me in the ass.

As Dante's fist connected with my jaw, I squeezed my eyes tight and breathed through my nose, through the pain that reverberated throughout my entire body. It was not the first time I'd been tortured, and I was sure it wouldn't be the last, but I knew how to handle the pain.

"We had a deal," Dante leaned down by my ear, whispering so the others didn't hear.

I spat the blood from my mouth onto the floor next to his feet.

I stared up at him through swollen eyes and did my best to glare.

"I'm well aware," I told him, not needing my memory to be refreshed about the deal I'd originally struck with Dante. Before the FBI had hired me, Dante had reached out first. He'd known the FBI would be needing my assistance in the near future, and he wanted to get ahead of it, by making me a double agent of sorts. He was always looking out for Emilia. I understood the why, but what I didn't understand was why he didn't tell her the truth. That was his cross to bear, not mine.

"Do you?" he questioned me. "You seem to have gone off course, and yet no results. Seems you've been distracted, hmm?"

"Last time I checked I haven't completed my mission yet, have I?" I taunted back. "And I always get the job done."

He didn't answer with words, instead a punch landed in my gut. I doubled over, gasping for air as the breath was knocked out of me.

"We should tell her, Dante. I hate lying to her," I said, spitting out more blood.

"I'm doing this to protect Emilia. She already has a lot on her plate. She cannot know about our deal."

It was then that I felt my skin prickle with electricity. I felt her before I saw her.

Dante went to speak, but I saw dark raven hair appear out of my peripheral vision.

"Enough," her voice came, soothing and calm. "Leave us, Dante."

He looked over at her and nodded his head in submission. When he turned back to me, his eyes bored into mine, and when he took a step back, he looked back at me, silencing our conversation for the time being.

He passed Emilia on the way out, squeezing her shoulder in warning as he left.

I peered over at Emilia as she strode into the room, hovering over me. I drank in my fill of her standing there, and from this angle she looked like an avenging angel. She still had her hair tied back in a tight ponytail, and wore a white tank top that fit tightly to her body with black pants hugging her curves. When my eyes finally traveled back up to her face, I found a look of vengeance directed at me. Her icy blue eyes glared down at me, and it was as if the temperature in the room dropped several degrees from the intensity of it. Her lethal look was chilling to the bone, and I felt my body shiver involuntarily. But despite the cool, hard mask she displayed currently, I could see beyond that cold exterior that she was hurt by my betrayal, more than she would let on.

*She threw a right hook at my face and my head snapped hard to the side.

"Why did you have to go and ruin it all?"

Another punch found its mark, and I felt my teeth rattle inside my mouth at the impact.

"I needed to see it for myself," I quietly muttered.

"Was my word not enough? You needed me to show you?" she let out a choked sob.

"No, it wasn't," I regrettably told her, my face falling at the truth in my words.

"Was any of it real?" she whispered, her voice hollow, almost ghost-like. "Or was everything a lie?"

"There's a quote I have grown to love," I stated, changing the topic. "There are two tragedies in life. One is to lose your heart's desire. The other is …"

"… To gain it," she finished.

I looked at her, eyes pleading as I discarded my heart onto the floor. "Have I lost it?"

She blinked once, then twice, and her mouth twitched briefly. Blink and I would've missed it, but I didn't. My words struck her, hitting home.

The more that I got to know Emilia over the last few months, I knew what she desired most. It wasn't to be feared or envied, but to be loved; deeply, passionately, and whole-heartedly. I wanted to be the one that gave that to her, because I knew deep down I couldn't stand another man in my place doing it.

---

* I Found - Amber Run

She opened her mouth to speak, her lips parting, but nothing ever came out.

"Emilia," I tried again, her name on my lips sounding like a prayer.

Hearing her name, she shook her head as if to clear the noise, and I felt the burn of hope in me die out to mere embers as she replied.

"You never gained it," she responded in a dull, bored voice. The despair spread throughout my chest at her dismissal, and I hung my head in defeat. But when I peeked at her, I watched as her delicate veil slipped slightly, and I saw the blatant lie written all over her features. I couldn't tell if it was my injuries finally catching up to me and I was just delirious from the blood loss, but I clung to that hope, that one moment she gifted me.

"Now what?" I half whispered, half croaked as I felt my body shutting down, needing rest.

I didn't hear what she said as I slipped under, and blackness blanketed my vision. The last thing I saw before I went under was her retreating figure as she left me alone once more.*

I was thrust back inside that building, my body on autopilot as I peered around corners and made myself invisible again. There are rows of wire shelving filling the room. I

---

* Stop playing I Found - Amber Run

was standing behind one of them when I saw her enter the room.

The look on her face was ravenous as she hunted down her prey. A man came out of nowhere and fired at her, but she moved and sent a bullet flying back, killing him in an instant.

The change in the air was staggering. The chaos around me died down to an eerie silence. Emilia's shoulders were tense as she dropped her head back, and I watched her lips as she mumbled something softly to herself. The second she heard her radio go off with her men all accounted for, I saw the physical release of relief fall from her shoulders.

It said a lot about Emilia's character. These men were her family, and I could tell she cared tremendously for each and every one of them. She radioed back to them, and then at the same time we both saw the man cowering in the dark make a beeline for the exit, but Emilia was faster and fired. I watched as the bullet found a home in the man's knee, but he retaliated and fired back at the same time Emilia dove toward the floor and pulled the trigger.

The man screamed in agony, but I couldn't care less. I moved along the shelf trying to get a better view of Emilia. She was sprawled out on the floor, and I knew I was about to blow my cover again. I went to make my way over to her, but she lifted her body off the floor and sank back on her heels. We both stared down at the tear in her sleeve on her left arm. I was filled with ease at the fact that it was just a graze.

My eyes traveled back up to her face, and she smiled wickedly down at her injury. She stood to her full height, still smiling viciously at her victim as she approached him.

I observed her from a distance as she leaned closer to him, digging her fingers deep into his bullet wound. He physically shook and his screams filled the air, and all the while Emilia's grin grew wider.

I couldn't hear what they were saying, and I couldn't get any closer without giving my position away, so I did my best to see what she did instead. The man reared his head back and spat in her face, and I felt my jaw tighten as my teeth ground down hard. *He's dead*, I thought, my hand curling into a tight fist.

In retaliation, she lifted his right hand and sawed off a finger.

I considered their exchange of words. The look of absolute hatred and malice in her eyes told me this wasn't just some man under Camila's reign, but rather a man she knew personally. Someone she hated deep down to her core.

He said something to her, and I watched as the light in her eyes dimmed to a dark, cool flame of resignation. She closed her eyes briefly, and when they opened, the Emilia I had come to know was gone. In her place was a true monster, the one that laid dormant beneath her skin. The monster people had come to fear unleashes and all I can do is watch as she carves this man's flesh from his skin like she's carving a pumpkin. I can see the man start to fade from the excruciating pain, but she hits him across the face, leaning forward to whisper something in his ear. When she's done and she comes back to sit on her heels, clutched tightly in her hand, is ... Dear God ... is that his spleen?

I was not sure how I felt at the sight of Emilia going full Dexter on the man before me. A part of me was absolutely terrified of the monster she kept caged, but the other side of me was equally turned on by the sheer violence.

And as she grabbed the katana sword from her back and came down hard on the man's neck, beheading him, my cock stood at full attention and I stared at her transfixed as she rearranged her victim into an original Emilia masterpiece.

And despite the monster that Emilia unleashed tonight, I was even more enthralled by who she was as a person. She had bewitched me, something no woman had done before. I'd kept my distance in the past, never getting close to women. They always wanted more, wanted to settle down, and that was never my style. But in that moment, looking at Emilia in her prime, I knew I'd give her whatever she asked of me.

As the memory of tonight swept me away in its current, I treaded water, trying to keep myself afloat. Instead of telling Emilia the truth tonight, I buried it deep within my chest cavity, praying it would never see the light of day. I had accused her of something so heinous and unforgivable that I'd ruined all the trust we had built. I should've told her she was captivating, enlightening, a beautiful powerhouse, but they were just words I never said, and now she was slipping through my fingers, and taking my heart with her.

CHAPTER TWENTY-SEVEN

MATTEO

My eyes blinked awake, and instantly I found that I was no longer alone. Emilia stood before me, her head cocked and a mischievous smile on her face. Her hair flowed wild and untamed down her back, its shine reflecting under the dimmed yellow lighting, and I'm lost briefly in her glow.

She stood before me in a simple and comfortable outfit of leggings and a white tee, no makeup on, and all I could think was that she'd never looked more beautiful.

"Welcome back to the land of the living," she chirped.

My head felt like an anvil was resting on top of it, and my eyes were swollen shut.

She continued before I could even find the words to respond to her.

"I thought you may want some company," she taunted.

It took all of the strength I had left to lift my head and look over to what her body had been concealing before.

To my right, Tobias's body hung limply, his wrists shackled to the iron cuffs that dangled from the ceiling. His bare feet just barely scraped the floor, and from what I could see, there was a bruise already starting to take shape on his face.

He was unconscious, but not for long.

Emilia walked over to his body as she continued to speak to me. "Maybe if I torture someone you care about, you'll tell me what I want to know."

She picked up a bucket that was located on the ground next to Tobias and threw the cold water on him.

I watched as he frantically came to, quietly but quickly taking in his surroundings and assessing the situation. His eyes widened when he saw that I was also detained in the room with him.

"Tobias," my voice croaked in defeat, my throat dry and raspy from lack of water.

I was not sure how long I'd been unconscious for; if I had to guess, a day probably had come and gone. Being underground with no windows or light made it hard to truly determine how much time had passed.

When I didn't check in with Tobias after the raid over at the docks, he probably came sniffing around, making it easy for Emilia to get to him.

"That's cruel, baby," I chastised her, faintly shaking my head, "You had me all to yourself, but three's a bit of a crowd, don't you think?" I lightly joked, trying to ease the tension in the room. Emilia could do whatever she wanted to me, and I'd deserve her wrath, but Tobias was just following orders. *My* orders. He didn't belong here.

A sinister smile fell upon her lips and the look she pinned me with was as cold as death as she simply responded to my light-hearted pleas.

"I guess we shall see, won't we?"

And with those words, she raised her hand that she had cloaked behind her and drew a knife across Tobias's exposed chest.

The blade ripped through his skin, the tattooed roses and vines that curled their way up his ribs and across his chest now dripping in red, like bloody thorns.

He didn't scream, but his eyes did with fury as they

narrowed to slits. His jaw clenched tight, and I knew he was seething inside.

I knew it was nothing he couldn't handle. He'd been through a lot worse. All of us had, so this torture he was enduring was child's play, but that didn't matter to him. His blood boiled beneath the surface and I sensed his resentment toward Emilia growing the more she carved into him.

"Tell me what I want to know, Matteo."

I sighed in defeat.

"Ok, Emilia," I told her exasperatedly. "I'll tell you whatever you want to know. Just—" I hesitated. "Point your knife at me. Take it out on me, not Tobias. This is between me and you," I told her.

"Mmm ... that's not how this works," she reprimanded me. "I'm going to ask you a question, and you're going to answer truthfully," she divulged, "and if you don't"—she brought her blade back towards Tobias's skin—"I carve a new wound into your friend here."

She began to dig the tip of the knife further into his skin, and I relented.

"Stop, Emilia, you're in control."

She hovered the knife over his chest as she asked me her first question.

"Who are you, really?"

It was simple and I might laugh if it weren't for the situation at hand. If the knife was directed at me, I would have laughed, but that was not the case here.

"My name is Matteo Ricci; that's not a lie," I stated. "The background check you ran on me was the truth. I do own a gun-for-hire business for those who can afford me, and before that, I was a soldier for the United States, and prior to that, you know I grew up in Italy. My life in Italy I had expunged from my files, yet you were able to find that, so compliments to you."

She pondered my answer for a minute or so, and I held

my breath waiting. She must find me truthful, because she didn't add to Tobias's injuries.

"Who hired you?"

She held my gaze steadily, and I forced myself to swallow, knowing this would be what destroyed her. Destroyed *us*.

Not being able to look Emilia in the eyes as I betrayed her once more, I hung my head in shame at my words as they pierced the still air.

"The FBI."

Two words.

That's all it took for me to lose her.

To lose everything.

I stared at the bloody floor underneath me, not enough of a man to face her, when I heard her storm over towards me. She gripped my hair, yanking my head so I was forced to meet her eyes.

Her eyes reminded me of the Adriatic Sea, and I was paralyzed in place, as they glistened with tears that she'd never let fall. The tears that crested in her eyes looked like waves on the ocean, and I had never hated myself more than I did in that moment.

"Why?" she grit out forcefully.

Why, she asks? Why did I betray her?

That was a good question, and truthfully, I had no good answer. I could've easily told her that it was her second that had hired me as a double agent. That I was a spy within the FBI in favor of her, but I knew that truth would break her more. If she were to find out the man she had grown up with and trusted the most had essentially betrayed her even though it was in her best interest, she'd be devastated, and I don't think their friendship would recover. So I took the blame, because before I met her, I'd never truly cared about anything besides getting paid and my car.

*I'd met her, and suddenly it was as if my world was saturated in vibrant colors. I tasted her, and I craved more of her body, but also her mind. I wished that I never had touched another woman before her, and I knew I'd kill the next that touched her in the same ways that I desired to.

Somewhere along the way of betraying her, I'd started to fall in love with Emilia DeLuca and everything she was—the powerhouse Chicago knew her as, the exposed version of her that kept her walls up but allowed me to slip in through a window, and even the demon she kept buried—-I fell in love with them all.

There was not a damn thing I'd change about Emilia, but now it was too late. It didn't matter what I wanted anymore. My heart felt like a live wire, as if I were wearing my skin inside out. One touch of her hand and I'd implode.

"You've been on their radar for a while now, but they've never been able to prove anything. They believed you were behind the human trafficking ring—"

"As did you," she spat out venomously, interrupting me.

I grimaced at her words, knowing it hurt her to speak them, but they hurt me more.

Guilt overwhelmed me, as well as the shame I felt knowing I was foolish to not have trusted her from the start.

"I know better now," I said.

My words meant little to her now, the damage already done.

"They intentionally put me on your radar in order to infiltrate your ranks. To get close to you, find out your secrets, your flaws."

I lost momentum in my admission as the gravity of what I'd done to her bore down on me in full force.

Her hold on me tightened as my words fully registered.

---

*   Tragic - Tommee Profitt, Fleurie

"And sleeping with me, was that part of their plan too?" she demanded.

"No!" I proclaimed, vigorously shaking my head, needing her to know that was not a lie. "That was me being selfish," I began to explain. "I was absolutely enthralled by you, and I needed to know you. You are unlike any woman I have ever met. The first time I touched you, it was like a fire ignited in my veins, and I know you felt it too. The second I tasted you, I knew it wouldn't be enough for me. Everything that transpired between us, Emilia, that was real. *We are real,*" I enunciated every word, needing her to hear the sincerity, the truth in my words.

She ripped her hand away, and my head fell forward with the momentum. I raised my head, trying to get a glimpse of any emotional response she may have had to my declaration, but I was not that lucky. She had her back turned and I attempted to read her body language, but failed. She was a closed book. She had shut me out.

Her shoulders lifted and fell with what felt like a defeated exhale, and I waited with bated breath. Emilia's voice was monotone and devoid of feeling when she turned to address me further.

"What did you give the FBI?"

I balked at her, completely thrown off kilter at her sudden disregard for me.

"Emilia."

Saying her name felt wrong, like I'd lost the privilege, but I was grasping at the last shred of hope I had.

"I know you feel the same," I whispered. "Don't do this," I begged.

She flinched, and a deeply pained look came across her face. Her eyes closed and her head hung in surrender. When her eyes found mine again they were lethal.

"Don't do this," she repeated back to me, shaking her

head, her mouth forming an "O." "I didn't do this, Matteo; *you* did. You did this to us."

"I'm falling in love with you, Emilia," I revealed, my words a desperate Hail Mary.

She reared back at the words in shock.

"You can't be shocked by that statement. I don't do love," I started to explain to her. "I didn't care about anything in my life besides my work, but then you happened. And suddenly I want everything that comes with the feeling of loving someone, loving you—whatever that entails for us."

Emilia's posture wavered, and I observed the vulnerability she revealed as a lone tear slid down her face.

I attempted one more time to earn her forgiveness, praying I was right about how she felt about me.

"And I know you love me too, despite what you may tell yourself."

"You're wrong, I don't love you," she whispered in a soft tone. "I'm indifferent toward you."

She stared past me, not daring to look me in the eyes because she knew if she did, I would catch her in her lie.

"I thought we didn't lie to each other. I told you before, you are many things, Emilia, a liar is not one of them."

"You never should have fallen for me."

"It's too late, I already have."*

Her eyes dropped to mine briefly, before turning back toward Tobias.

"What does the FBI know?" she redirected her question, shutting down our conversation indefinitely.

Tobias remained silent, and I wanted to throttle him for his obedience. We were trained in torture, how to withstand it and how to do it. He was built for this, and he would die before he gave up any information.

---

* Stop playing Tragic - Tommee Profitt, Fleurie

Not wanting her to use her knife on him again, I answered for him.

"Nothing concrete," I said. "They know about the weapons trafficking and money laundering as well as the extortion, but they can't prove anything. What they're after, though, is the human trafficking ring they think you're operating."

Her focus remained on Tobias as she replied.

"Which you have seen firsthand that I don't."

"The FBI doesn't care about that. They are willing to pin this on you and make it stick so they can get you on your other crimes. You are the big fish they want to reel in," I told her.

She contemplated this for a bit before she whipped her head back toward me.

"What if I give them a bigger fish? Someone who they may want more than me."

I mulled that over, debating if that may work, but Tobias finally decided to break his silence and answered instead.

"They won't take the deal. They're not willing to negotiate with you."

She glanced over at him, a smile playing at her lips.

"Good, because I don't cooperate with feds."

She pivoted and started to stride toward the door with purpose, pulling out her cell phone as she did.

"You can't run from this, Emilia," Tobias said.

Emilia stopped at the door, her hand frozen on the handle.

"I don't run, I never did," and with those parting words she left us alone with our thoughts.

CHAPTER TWENTY-EIGHT

EMILIA

*I SLAMMED THE DOOR SHUT BEHIND ME, MY PHONE CRADLED in my hand. I took in a deep breath and allowed myself ten seconds to feel every emotion from that conversation with Matteo. I glanced back through the closed door as if I could still see him strapped to the chair, pouring his heart out to me.

He knew me well enough by now to know everything I said was a lie. Without meaning to, I'd carelessly let the enemy into my home, into my bed, and even into my heart. My mind and heart volleyed back and forth between that term: *enemy*. Was he my enemy, truly?

He was a gun-for-hire, and it made sense that the FBI would have him deep in their claws, but what didn't make sense was Matteo knew the bodies I'd buried and could put me behind prison bars once more, but he hadn't. If he had told the FBI everything I had confided in him, I had a feeling agents would have already been spilling into this house, but that certainly wasn't the case.

So that left the question: whose side was Matteo truly on?

A part of me did believe that the feelings between us were

---

* I Love You - Billie Eilish

real. Just as I had spilled my guts to him, he had done the same with me. Matteo Ricci was a man that kept his cards close to his chest and had an emotional wall as tall as the Great Wall of China, but he'd carved a hole in the wall for me to climb through. He exposed his vulnerability to me, and he didn't do that lightly.

But how I felt, *no, had felt*, about Matteo Ricci, I buried deep inside where hopefully this time it would stay entombed in its coffin, never to see the light of day again.

I placed my other hand on the door and brought my forehead to rest on the cold, solid surface before me trying to rein in my thoughts. Whatever this was between me and Matteo would have to wait. In another life, I would have just been an ordinary woman who met a normal handsome guy at a party, but that wasn't who I was, that wasn't who we were. That was a fantasy that I couldn't afford to dwell in. With one last deep breath, I exhaled a muted sigh and with it expelled all thoughts of Matteo.

Lifting my head high, I turned and made my way down the hallway away from the door holding Matteo and Tobias. Even though the door was solid steel and soundproof, I couldn't risk anyone hearing the conversation I was about to have.

Pulling up the contacts in my phone, I dialed the number I'd been putting off calling. My thumb hovered over the green call icon, but not for long. With nothing left to lose, I hit send and brought the phone to my ear. It rang only once before someone on the other line picked up.

"I'm ready to accept my role in the *Septem Daemonia*," I told the listener on the other end, having a feeling it was the man I'd met just weeks ago.

I could almost feel him smiling on the call when he said,

"Welcome, Miss DeLuca, we'll be in touch," and with dramatic flair he ended the call.*

Once again, I found myself back in the same parking garage on the fifth level. And I had déjà vu, because not a car was in sight. This time there was no Glock resting heavy in my lap, nor was I picking at my cuticle beds like a frightened little girl. I had accepted my fate for what it was. There was no getting out of this life; the only way to leave the mafia world was in a body bag. And if there was anybody that was ending up there, it was Camila, and I wouldn't bury her six feet under. No, I'd much rather she sink to the bottom of the ocean, as far down as she could possibly go.

I took a quick glance in my rearview mirror and applied my lip gloss as if it were somehow a shield that would protect me from whatever was to happen. I stepped out of my car, my boots barely grazing the ground when I heard the sound of an approaching car.

An armored Escalade drove down the open lane and stopped nearly five feet from where I stood in an outfit dressed to kill. My long legs extended toward the sky in my tall black boots. I wore a slim-fitting black dress and matching tights, and with my oversized black leather trench coat draped around me, I was everything this city painted me as, *the Black Widow.*

---

*   Stop playing I Love You - Billie Eilish

189

LESLIE BATES

The SUV's high beams stretched their fingers out toward me, but I didn't dare move an inch to shield my eyes from the brightness. I stood firmly in place, my head held high as I waited for them to make the first move.

After a minute, the back door opened and slammed shut, and I was face to face once more with the same stranger I met just months ago.

"Miss DeLuca," he said in a silvery voice, stepping in front of one of the car's headlights. The man is dressed in an elegant grey tailored suit that matches his salt and pepper hair. His warm brown eyes like melted chocolate meet mine as he continues. "I'm so glad you called."

He stepped forward until we were a few feet apart. This close to him I could see the more minute details of his appearance. His eyes were soft and inviting, yet tired and with heavy eye bags. His smile was well-practiced and a little wrinkled. He was the perfect guy to send because he looked like the generous type and trustworthy. He reminded me of a therapist that you'd find sitting in one of those brown leather chairs in a stuffy office with a tweed jacket and loafers. Talking to them was like drinking hot chamomile on a cold winter day, and suddenly you were willing to delve deep into your childhood trauma and voice your deepest, darkest secrets.

The *Septem Daemonia* definitely knew what they were doing when they hired him, but I wasn't going to take the bait.

"Yes, we meet again," I responded, waiting for him to fill in the gaps.

"Ah, my apologies, Miss Deluca. I'm Benjamin, but you can call me Benji," he volunteered, offering me his hand. I took the offered handshake, finally satisfied with putting a name to the face.

"Step into my office." He gestured to the waiting car. "We have much to discuss. And something tells me you already need the *Septem Daemonia's* help," Benji said with a knowing smile.

I didn't respond with words, but rather a tight-lipped smile as I stepped toward the now open back door. I mentally took a moment to myself before stepping into the car and the conversation that would soon follow.

I was greeted by the scent of black ice air freshener and the stale air of men's cologne when the car door shut behind me. I muffled my choking at the onslaught of smells with a subtle clearing of my throat as I settled into the plush leather seats. I took in my surroundings as I attempted to get comfortable. The seats were black with red stitching trailing alongside the edges, and in the corner I saw refreshments that ranged from water, and coffee to a bottle of Dame. Benji must have seen me glance over at the drinks, because he was quick to offer me a glass.

"I'm good, thank you though," I said, my polite business woman side coming out to make an appearance.

He politely smiled over at me, before turning his body to face me more directly.

I didn't wait for him to take control of the conversation, so I just dove right in.

"How does this work exactly?" I prompted. "I just sign my name on the imaginary dotted line to the devil and then we're both richer and more powerful than before?"

"Right to business I see." He clapped his hands together for effect. "Not exactly," he started. "As I mentioned to you when we first met, the *Septem Daemonia* is interested in you for many reasons. You are a powerhouse in this city and it's a title you have earned. The members of this secret society are wealthy, powerful, and influential people with ties to everything you can imagine. The invitation that was originally sent out to you was a preliminary initiation," he explained.

My mind drifted to when I'd first received their cryptic invitation. I had just returned from working out downstairs, and there, sitting ominously on my pillow, was a gold envelope tied together with a black ribbon. Curious as to what it was,

I'd pulled the carefully curated bow apart and read the invitation.

Inside was an invitation to the exclusive secret society of the *Septem Daemonia*. I remember standing there shell-shocked at seeing the words of the secret society's name clearly written out in my hands. I had only heard whispers about it in the streets. When you are a powerful figure in this city, you come across the hushed rumors circulating the underground circuit. But that was all that I had thought they were——-rumors. This invitation felt like a heavy weight in my hands, and it felt very much real to me. Included in their invitation, it had mentioned my first task of initiation was to throw a party worthy of the attention of the *Septem Daemonia*. If there was anything I knew how to do, it was throw a party. And in bold letters written in elegant calligraphy at the bottom were the words *choose a sin to embody*."

"The second step was piquing your interest further, which was when I contacted you days after your party," Benji continued, pulling me out of my memory.

"I merely gave you crumbs as to what the *Septem Daemonia* can offer you, knowing that in due time the curiosity of it all would eventually drive you to make that phone call."

"All you're telling me is that this secret society is powerful and has an extended reach worldwide. I am already a powerful and rich woman. Why do you assume that money and power are something I'd crave more of? I'm not a man," I told him matter-of-factly. "I didn't get to where I am today because I envied the money or status."

He laughed at my remark. "I love your ferocity and boldness. I never said you craved more of those things, Miss DeLuca, just simply indicated that those were some of the benefits we had to offer. No, what you crave is *security*."

My smile twitched just slightly. To others, none would be the wiser, but someone like Benji, who saw everything, caught my little slip and it told him everything he needed to confirm why I was here. He knew he hit it right on the head.

I did crave security. Not in my status of power or finances but in life. I wanted to feel safe, or as safe as I could be given the life I led. The criminals that tried their luck to take a hit at me were amateurs and came with the job description. I craved security from Camila and her cartel, and I had a feeling Benji knew this and was counting on that.

"Join us, Miss DeLuca, and the world is at your fingertips. We know you have the feds breathing down your neck, and we can handle that easily with just one phone call."

He studied my face, for what I wasn't sure, but I didn't change my facial expression or give anything away so easily.

"Something tells me though that's not your biggest threat, am I right?"

I didn't play into his taunts or the game he was trying to play to get me to falter.

"You had mentioned last time that we had a common enemy—who?" I demanded.

"We would have thought you had figured it out by now."

I looked at him, not revealing anything in my face, but the next words out of his mouth shocked me to my core.

"Does the name *La Corredora* ring any bells?"

"And if it does?"

"Then this next piece of information may pique your interest. Not too long ago, the *Septem Daemonia* had made a deal with Camila. She would smuggle her drugs into the United States and we'd get a cut."

I interrupted him, my voice scathing, not caring if I came across as rude.

"So you knew about her sex trafficking?" I accused him.

"We didn't become aware of her side business until you escaped from her clutches. She had gone off-book. And while we are not saints, we do not condone the sale of humans," he said with conviction.

"I'd like her gone, and I'm not talking about gone as in out of my city. I want her dead. I've been stripping her power apart slowly over the years, but it's not enough. I need more assistance," I bit out the last word as if it was poison on my tongue. I hated having to admit to anyone, especially a man like Benji, that I need help. I was not the type of person to seek help.

I'd been burned too many times in my life to expect someone to help me out of the kindness of their heart, or to think that help won't come without a price. I'd lived thirty-two years fending for myself. Every time I needed help, screamed for it until my throat was bleeding and my voice hoarse, it never arrived. Which is how I became my own savior. So, asking for help, well, that didn't sit well in my stomach. It felt bitter coming out of my mouth, but at this point I knew it was necessary.

If joining this secret society would help handle this matter, then I'd put my bruised ego to the side and swallow my pride and sign my soul away.

"Consider it the first thing the *Septem Daemonia* does for you to ensure we have your best interests at heart. And in return, we would like you to dismantle the sex trafficking ring, but take over the drug smuggling."

I leaned back in my seat at what the secret society wanted from me.

"I don't dabble in drugs," I said.

"But you do smuggle in weapons, don't you?"

I may have smuggled in weapons that were hard to obtain, but I usually sold them for double the price to the military. Drugs were different.

"You must be prepared, Miss DeLuca, to do whatever it takes."

If I could take out Camila with the help of the secret society and take over her business and make it into something of mine, that'd be the ultimate revenge. Before I could back out of my decision, I stared at him with pure determination.

"Where do I sign?"

CHAPTER TWENTY-NINE

MATTEO

THE SECOND EMILIA CLOSED THE DOOR BEHIND HER, I HUNG my head once more in regret, happy to wallow here in my self-pity and misery. But Tobias didn't make it that easy for me.

"You're a goddamn fool," he said in a patronizing tone.

My head swiveled in his direction at his words. He continued his lecture to me as soon as he saw that he had my attention.

"You're also a fucking hypocrite, Matteo," he spat out at me like venom. "When you first started this business of yours, you ingrained into all of our heads that under no circumstances are we to mix business with pleasure. That we put the mission above everything, so imagine my surprise when I came to learn about your extracurricular activities with the target."

"Tobias, it's not …"

"It's not what, Matteo," he interrupted. "Were you going to say it's not what it looks like? It's not what you think? It's not the same? What is going to be your excuse, Matteo?" he yelled at me, the chains rattling in place from all the motion.

"I have no excuse, okay, Tobias. I fucked up, is that what you want me to say here?" My voice raised in the heat of the moment. "I got in too deep with Emilia, and I can't turn back now, I'm …"

"Don't say it," he pleaded.

"I'm in love with her, man," I admitted. "I never had anyone in my life to give a shit about after my mom died until I met the guys. You were all I had left, and because of what happened out in Afghanistan, I had made a promise to myself that I wouldn't allow myself to get close to anyone. I barricaded myself into a small, tight box and slammed the doors shut because I couldn't risk loving someone again for fear of losing them. Losing the guys that day broke me, Tobias, and because of that, I made that rule."

"You act as if you are the only one that lost them, Cap. I was there too. I almost died alongside them. I carry that burden every day too."

"I know, Tobias, but *you* didn't give them the order. I did. My hands are stained with their blood. It was *me* that had to tell Hannah that her fiancé was never coming home to see her walk down the aisle. It was *me* that informed Catherine that she was now a widow and would have to raise two children without a father. And it was *me* that had to tell Olivia that unfortunately her husband would not be returning home to her. Not only did I get my men killed, but I destroyed *families,* Tobias, because I didn't listen to my gut. I blindly followed the orders given to me, and I was negligent in carrying them out."

Tears ran down my face, and even if I could wipe them away, I wouldn't. I couldn't hide this pain anymore. Tobias tracked the movement with his eyes, and I could tell he was emotional as well.

"You never had to do that alone."

I shook my head. "Yes. I did," I told him.

He didn't answer me for a good amount of time. I soon realized it was because he was hesitating to ask his next question.

"Why her?"

He didn't ask me in a cruel, menacing way. I snuck a glance over his way and read his face. There was no anger or malice in his tone when he asked , he was just a friend asking why his friend loved a girl. He was genuinely curious.

"She's everything," I quietly whispered back.

I thought more about my answer, but it didn't take me long to follow up on his question.

"She's beautiful, and I'm not talking about her appearance. She's stunning, yes. But, working for her these past few months, I've had the privilege of getting to know Emilia the person, not Emilia the head of the DeLuca clan. She cares deeply about the people who work for her. She knows their names, their families, their passions, likes, dislikes. They are family to her. She took the loss of her men hard."

I paused, sighing heavily at knowing that I was part of why she lost Ricardo and Miguel in the first place. As cliché as it sounded, I was a different person then. I was a man hellbent on doing his job with no emotion. But then Emilia had taunted Tobias into firing, and I knew I had to step in to defuse the situation. When I'd tackled her out of the way, she peered up at me with wide and surprised oceanic blue eyes, and I was transfixed. Our eyes had locked, and I couldn't have looked away even if I wanted to. If she was a siren, then I was the naive sailor getting lost in those eyes until she drowned me.

"She comes off as this strong, independent woman because she has to be. She can't afford to show any sign of weakness in her line of work. But deep down she's a scared little girl who feels everything. She's not the soulless monster this city believes she is. She's empathetic towards people, and despite some of the things she's done in her past, I know she's a good person.

She's not the one trafficking women, Tobias. She's infiltrating these dens and saving the women. She gives them a brand new life and funds for them," I told him, pride pouring out of me in waves.

"That's incredibly selfless of her to do," he said.

"It is," I agreed, "and she doesn't gloat about it either. She doesn't ask for the recognition. She does it because it's the right thing to do."

"Then why does the FBI believe she's the one behind it all?"

That was a good question. It was a question I'd been asking myself a lot lately.

"That's what I'd like to know."

He went quiet again for a bit, but he then asked in a quiet, serious cadence.

"You really are in love with her?"

I lifted my head high and looked my best friend in the eye and, with no hesitation, I answered, "I am. I'm in love with Emilia. There was a time that I would have laid down my life for my men, and I still would for you, but now, Emilia has fallen into that category and there's not a goddamn thing I wouldn't do to protect her."

I spoke in a soft, serious manner when I told Tobias the next part.

"She silences the demons in my head, Tobias. When I'm with her, I hate myself less and less. I start to feel more like a man again in her presence, a man that is worthy enough to be with her. She makes me feel whole. It's like I was drowning all of these years and she ripped me from the current and gave me my first breath of fresh air." My words trailed off at my declaration.

He shook his head, chuckling into his chest.

"Oh man," he laughed. "Never thought I'd live to tell the tale of my boy in love."

The chains shook and swayed with his laughter.

I couldn't help but laugh at that statement as well. Once upon a time, I had been a man who didn't believe in love for myself. Never thought I would be deserving of it, really. I was content with a nomadic single life. Back then I was lucky if I remembered the name of the woman in my bed the morning after, but now, all I saw in my bed was Emilia's bare face and warm naked body pressed to mine. I savored that image for a bit, relishing in that memory and despising the fact that it was only days ago that was my reality. Now, my future doesn't look so bright.

"Do you think I lost her completely?"

I didn't even care how that sounded coming out. If Tobias thought I sounded like a whiny teenager who just found out his crush didn't like him back, he didn't show it. And frankly, I didn't give a fuck if he did. The thought of losing Emilia, especially to my lies, was unbearable.

The thing I loved about Tobias was that he was not one to sugarcoat the truth; he told you how it was and he did so very bluntly, albeit sometimes rudely.

"Honestly, I don't know. What I do know is that she is in love with you too."

My ears perked up at that.

"How do you know?"

He looked over at me, dumbfounded, as if I should have already known the answer to my question, but he appeased me anyway with his reply.

"The look on her face wasn't because she felt betrayed by you. Her face was in pain because she's in love with you and she was devastated by you deceiving her. No woman is that emotional and hurt over some guy she's sleeping with, unless she has true feelings for him."

I mulled over his perception of the situation, and a small spark of hope lit in my chest. I vowed to myself that I would do whatever it took to win her back. I would convince her that I wanted her for however long she would have me—forever was my hope—or I'd die trying.

"So now what do we do?" Tobias asked from across the room.

I dropped my head back, lost in my thoughts, unsure about anything at this point for the first time in my life.

"I don't know," I told him truthfully. "But for now, we wait."

We didn't see Emilia again for two days.

CHAPTER THIRTY

EMILIA

THERE WAS A LOT I HAD TO THINK ABOUT OVER THE NEXT FEW days. Between Matteo's many overwhelming confessions and my conversation with Benji about the *Septem Daemonia* and everything it entailed, I felt like I was at an impasse in my life.

Benji's solution to my current predicament sat heavily on my mind as I pondered every angle of how things could go exponentially wrong, but in hindsight it was the best resolution.

I went through my day on autopilot. I spoke with my men about the proceedings of my current businesses, made appearances at the club and the bar, all the while lost in my own tortured thoughts. I avoided Matteo at all costs. I needed more time, even though I knew I was limited on that as well.

I gave myself two days before I knew I had to go down there and face him. I stood there on the other side of the door staring blankly into the void. I let my mask slip and inhaled shakily, feeling my heart rattle inside my chest before I laid eyes on Matteo once again.

I didn't want to believe him; truly, I didn't. I never wanted to face the feelings I had for him. We were having fun, and that was it. In his words we were *using* each other for the other's body. No harm, no foul when there were no emotions attached. But he was right, and I hated him for that. I hated the fact that he was right because the truth was I was lying to myself.

It was easier to lie to myself and continue being ignorant, rather than admit out loud to myself the intense feelings I had for him. I was a fool for falling for him. People like me couldn't have *real* relationships. It was dangerous, and I wasn't stupid. I was well aware that Matteo also flirted with danger as well. That wasn't what scared me the most. Love was the greatest thing one could experience in life, and growing up I had always craved that. Hoping that maybe one day I'd find that special someone despite the life I was born into. But I never got to live a normal life. I was forced to grow up way too young and had my childhood innocence ripped from me.

After enduring those dark years, I gave up on that notion. All I ever would know for the rest of my life were monsters and death.

But when I looked at Matteo, I saw an equal. He was my mirror in every way. He wasn't afraid to get his hands stained with blood or to shoot first and ask questions later. He was confident and too good looking and he knew it, but he was also selfless. I know without a doubt he would've endured whatever torture came his way, taken beating after beating from my men. I knew this about him, which is why I knew his only military buddy would be his Achilles heel. After hearing him talk about that night and the men he lost, the one other person who'd survived that ambush besides him would be his weakness.

I saw Matteo cringe and his face contort with anguish as I carved my knife into his friend's chest. He gave himself up so quickly in the hope that I would inflict the pain on him instead. In that one move, he had told me everything. He folded like a house of cards—it was that easy. I should've done worse to Tobias for what he had done to Ricardo and Miguel.

I figured that out soon after Matteo revealed his true agenda. Before Matteo, I would've done worse, but it was because of him that I didn't. He couldn't see that day from where he was tied up, but I noticed Tobias's eyes tracking my hand movement and how it shook slightly at Matteo's words. Tobias read me that quickly and knew his words were eating me up inside despite the brave face I put on.

As riveting as it may sound, love was a weapon. Some may think it was the greatest strength, and while that may be true, it was also a person's biggest weakness. Matteo was a wall and would've withstood torture as he was trained to do for however long until his body gave up, but any secret he held inside his mind would've died along with him. But his love for Tobias made him weak, and now, unfortunately, I was his other weakness. As he was mine.

And I can't have him be my weakness.

I bent over slightly so the scanner could sweep over my eyes for recognition. When I heard the telltale beep and the green light appeared, I turned the handle and walked into my nightmare.

The first thing I noticed when I walked into the room was the heavy bags under Matteo's eyes. He looked a little worse for wear with the dark purple bruising on his face and a split lip. His blood was caked into his olive skin, which was currently layered with a sheen of dirt. The minute I stepped into the room and assessed him, his green eyes blinked open, and in them I watched as they drank in the sight of me. They reminded me of seaglass that I would find on the beach when I was a child. They penetrated through me, causing goose-bumps to rise on my skin.

He blinked away his sleepiness and his eyes opened a little bit wider, studying me as if he could read my thoughts as to where I had been the last few days.

"Hi," he whispered hoarsely.

I stared over at him in silence, not knowing what to say to him at this point. I gave him a brief nod and dove right into what I have to say.

"I'm letting you go," I announced to the men in the room.

Tobias looked over at me in shock, but it was Matteo's face I read as I spoke. He looked confused by my response after keeping them holed up for days.

"We're at war, and you're worth more to me out there than tied up in here," I stated matter-of-factly.

I moved the stepladder over to where Tobias stood and pulled out a key to unlock him from his chains. Once one arm was released, it hung limply by his side and when I moved over to his other hand to release him completely, he almost toppled over to the ground but regained his balance. He rubbed his arms absentmindedly as I made my way over to where Matteo sat, a look of bewilderment still etched into his features.

From my jeans, I pulled out a knife and delicately slid it between his bruised, chafed wrists and yanked upwards on the zip ties, freeing his hands. I circled to the front and unbound his legs, and all the while he gazed at me trying to read me. We stared at each other for a moment in our silent language, until Tobias broke the quiet.

"What do you mean by that?"

His voice shook me out of my reverie, and I stood up tall, mask slid back into its rightful place.

"If the FBI wants me, they're going to have to come and

LESLIE BATES

get me," I stated plainly. "But the FBI is not my main concern. It's Camila. If she wants a war, then she's going to get one."

"Are you sure provoking the head of a Mexican cartel is a great idea?"

I looked over at Tobias in disbelief.

"No more than provoking the head of an Italian mafia was a great idea, yet here you two still stand," I threw back at him.

He went silent at that statement. Matteo still hadn't spoken up since I released him. He was standing at this point, leaning his weight on the chair before him.

When he finally made eye contact with me again, his voice was devoid of emotion.

"Where does that leave us?"

I considered his question for a bit before squaring my shoulders and informing them of my plan. When I was done filling them in, Tobias was looking over at me with shocked eyes, and Matteo was glaring daggers. I knew he wouldn't like this plan, knowing that it would put me in the line of fire, but he didn't get a say.

"Emilia," he began, but I cut him off before he could finish.

"My mind is made up, Matteo. We each have our parts to play, and if you really want to prove to me that all of what transpired between us wasn't a lie, then you'll do as I ask."

His expression sobered and his eyes went cold, but he didn't argue with me.

"Good." I made my way over to the door and knocked twice and stepped back as it swung forward, revealing the on call doctor.

"Dr. Ward will look over your injuries."

I then looked over to my doctor and addressed him directly. "Tend to their wounds and make sure they're all good. I'll be needing their abilities in a day's time."

And with those parting words, I shut the door behind me.

206

When Dante found me hours later, I was sitting in my home office poring over my books and I had newspaper articles scattered over my dark oak desk.

He wasted no time in informing me about the status of Matteo and Tobias.

"Dr. Ward patched them up, and they are good to go. Tobias has already left the premises, but before he left, he said he'd be there tomorrow."

I didn't bother to look at Dante when I answered, praying that my tone of voice was nonchalant when I asked, "And Matteo?"

I heard his agitated sigh as he answered.

"He remains here at the estate. He was pretty insistent that he stay here in fact. He refused treatment by the doctor unless I agreed to the terms."

I peeked a glance up at Dante, and he looked at me in that older brother way of his, like he knew all my secrets. He stared back at me knowingly, but I didn't think that warranted a response. Instead, in my usual fashion, I changed the topic completely.

"Dante, you've been with me my whole life, and words can't explain how truly grateful I am to have you in my life."

His eyebrows pinched together, and he looked at me quizzically.

"Why are you talking like this, Emmy?"

I skated over his words and continued with what I had to say. If I didn't say this now, then I never would. It was a conversation that I wished I would never have to have, but I knew was absolutely necessary.

"If something should happen to me tomorrow ..."

"Don't talk like that!" he interrupted. "You know any one of us would die for you, Emilia. Nothing will happen to you tomorrow, I swear on my life."

I gave him a warm smile of gratitude in return. Dante had always been so loyal to me and my family, and I had always cherished the bond we had formed over the years. When he had found me after my escape, he had informed me that he never gave up trying to track me down. It was Dante that had picked me up that night from Romeo's burning house. He didn't ask questions. Not about the blood that I was coated in or the flames licking the skyline behind me. He just simply asked if I was hurt, and when I shook my head in response, he squeezed my hand and put the car in gear.

"You know better than to make a promise you may not be able to keep." I tried to laugh to defuse the tension, but he looked anything but thrilled. "If something were to happen," I started again and this time he let me finish, as he silently shook his head at the thought. "I need you to continue this fight. My fight. If Camila were to win tomorrow, you must continue to keep her out of this city. You have to be the one to take over saving those girls. For me." My voice croaked on the last few words.

He knew better than to argue with me about any of this.

"I promise I'll carry on the fight."

When he knew I was satisfied with his answer, I moved on.

"Now that has been settled, I have business to discuss with you. Have you seen this?" I asked him, tossing one of the newspaper articles over to his side of the desk. He picked up the piece of paper, where I had already marked the article I wanted him to read over. I watched as his eyes widened slightly and then crinkled, and I knew what he must be recognizing.

When he was done reading the article, he looked over at me with surprise.

"The *Angel of Death*, huh? That's what they are calling this vigilante?"

"Indeed, they are, and it's very fitting. Some are calling for her head; others are saying she's a hero. I happen to agree with the latter," I told him.

He looked at me with curiosity. "How do you know it's a woman?"

I gave him a calculating smile. "Ever heard of the name Gianna Hayek?"

"The criminal lawyer?"

"I want you to find her and bring her to me. I have something to discuss with her."

"Emilia," he started off. "You honestly think this lawyer is the vigilante they're talking about?"

I didn't reveal how I knew, but I knew it was her.

"Gianna Hayek, Dante," I said, grabbing the newspaper back from him. "Find her."

CHAPTER THIRTY-ONE

MATTEO

I paced back and forth in my room so many times I think I left an imprint in the rug. The sight of Emilia after two days of not seeing her fucked me up in ways I couldn't even describe. I'd bared my soul to her, which was something in itself. I was not an emotional person, and yet there I was practically throwing my heart at her, only for her to disappear. I got a brief taste of my own medicine in that sense. Now I understood how women felt when I had ghosted them after sex.

When I awoke to Emilia inside that bare room, I thought I was hallucinating. I didn't know where we stood after my confession to her days ago, but when she released me and we made eye contact, something about her had changed significantly. Her blue eyes were devoid of vibrancy, and she overall just seemed exhausted.

As soon as she revealed her plan to me and Tobias, all I saw was red. I gripped the chair in front of me that had kept me prisoner for half a week so tightly, my knuckles turned a stark white. She was putting herself in unnecessary danger, and there was nothing I could do to prevent her from following through with this foolish half-baked plan.

I didn't mutter a single word after Emilia left, not when Tobias tried to coax me into a conversation and certainly not when her doctor looked me over. After a few feeble attempts at getting me to talk, he gave up and settled for non-verbal grunts or simple shakes of the head. I finally spoke when Dante walked into the room. After he dismissed the doctor after checking in with him about how we were and telling Tobias he was free to go, he finally addressed me.

Alone once more with no one else in the vicinity, we were able to finish our conversation from before. By the end of our conversation, we could agree on one thing: neither of us was pleased by Emilia's *brilliant* plan. However, I did request that if I was to go through with this, that I was staying here. Selfishly, I just didn't want to leave her side.

Every slight sound in the house had me holding my breath, listening for her footsteps in the hall, but the only noise I heard was the far-off thunder from the open windows. I stood there, my ears straining for any movement, my eyes focused on the door as I stood there in the dark, the moon as my guard as it illuminated the open space before me.

I let out a groan of agitation. I'd been back in my room for hours now and besides the hour-long hot shower I treated myself to, I've done nothing but stare at this door. I knew I could've gone and actively sought her out, but I didn't want to pressure her. I wanted her to come to me. I pulled my phone out of my back pocket and ignored the multiple text messages sent by Tobias, and zeroed in on the time.

12:54 am.

My hope was wearing thin, but just when I was going to give up for the night, I heard the telltale sign of her tiny feet padding across the bare wood outside. In two giant steps, I was already across the room and swinging my door open only to find Emilia with her hand half raised, poised to knock on my door.

"Hi."*

All the things I wanted to say to her, and all I could come up with was a simple two-letter word.

"Hi," she breathed out. She shook her head, her face contorting into confusion. "I don't know why I'm here," she said, but I think it was mostly to herself.

"I think you do."

The words were barely out of my mouth when Emilia came crashing over the threshold and into my arms. The kiss wasn't delicate, it was passionate and messy. Our tongues fumbled in the dark, our hands searching for each other to bring us closer. I brought my hand up to twine through her hair, and I gripped the back of her head, deepening our kiss.

And just when I began to think I had her back, she pulled away from me, and I heard the slap across my face before I felt the searing pain in my cheek. She staggered backward away from me, her hand flying to her mouth as if her lips were on fire. She seemed stunned.

I started to approach her cautiously as if she were a scared stray. One wrong move and she'd flee.

She threw her hand up to stop me and I halted in my tracks, anxiously waiting for what would happen next. She caught her breath for a few seconds, and when she finally regained her composure, the next three words out of her mouth tore me apart.

"I hate you."

Three words and I was incapacitated.

"Emilia," I pleaded, edging closer but with each step toward her, she took a step back.

"No. I need to say this, or I never will."

I put up my hands in surrender to show her I was listening and not moving any closer, I was giving her space. Once she seemed satisfied with that, she took up pacing back and forth,

---

* We Go Down Together - Billie Eilish

tracing the very line I previously did for hours. I lifted the corner of my lip slightly when she turned away at how similar we were, but it was gone by the time she faced me again.

"I don't trust easily," she started, "I …" she stumbled on her next words and hearing the catch in her voice broke me. I wanted to shelter her from the pain, not be the one who caused it.

"I once believed that maybe someone like me could have something close to what society calls love, but I knew it was a fool's hope."

She went silent, staring out the window, as thunder cracked through the sky, causing the estate to shake, and immediately after lightning struck outside and painted Emilia in a haunting manner.

"You started to give me hope again," she choked out. She came at me, her fists flying, punching me in the chest rapidly. "I trusted you!" she screamed.

I took her punches, every blow. God, what I'd give to take all of that pain from her.

"And you betrayed me! Why!" she screamed, her fists losing momentum. "Why?" she said sobbing into my chest, her tears coming and soaking my t-shirt.

I pulled her in close and held her, one hand wrapped protectively around her lower back, the other buried in her hair. I tried to soothe her by humming an old song my mom used to sing to me. We stood there in that embrace for what felt like hours, but honestly I would have stayed there in that moment cradling her in my arms for months if it meant I could relieve her of the pain I caused her.

Her whimpers slowly fade and she finally speaks up.

"That sounded beautiful."

Her voice is muffled by my shirt but I understood her clear as day. She looked up at me with her tear-streaked face, and I've never felt so low.

"What was it?"

I absentmindedly ran my hand through her locks of hair, gently brushing away the few strands that stuck to her face from her tears.

"It's *Make You Feel My Love* by Bob Dylan," I told her. "My mother would sing it to me when I was a child. I was plagued with nightmares even back then, and strangely enough, it was that song that would help me sleep. I thought it might help, but …"

"Thank you."

I knew she hadn't forgiven me, but those two words, though it may sound silly, breathed hope in me. I didn't trust my voice not to break, so instead I kissed her forehead in response.

I left my lips pressed to her forehead when I conveyed my thoughts to her.

"I'm not asking you to forgive me now, but I hope in time you can."

I pulled back and gazed down at her, making sure she could see the look of regret but truth in my words. "Just know I plan to spend every breath fighting to win you back, to show you that I'm worth it, that *we're* worth it. I don't care if it's months or if it takes me the rest of my life, but I'm in this with you, Emilia. Where you go, I will follow. You jump off a cliff, I'm standing by your side holding your hand. You run into the lion's den, I'll cover your six."

I placed both my hands on her cheeks and kept our eyes locked.

"You're it for me, Emilia. I'm yours."*

The words had no sooner left my mouth when Emilia lifted onto her toes and kissed me. I felt the soft brush of her lips on mine and then she was pushing her tongue into my mouth, and fuck, had I missed her taste. Her kiss tasted like whiskey and salt from her tears and it was perfect. She used

---

* Stop playing We Go Down Together - Billie Eilish

her body to push me backward until the backs of my knees hit the edge of the bed. The second they did, she maneuvers me down onto the bed and straddled my thighs. My hands glided up her body, and for the first time I took her in completely. When she first came in, I was too enraptured by the fact that she was there and kissing me. Now, I wanted to drink my fill. My hands skimmed across tights the same shade as her perfect hair, until my fingertips found purchase on the bottom of her black pencil skirt, a daring slit right in the middle. Both my eyes and hands traveled north to her flowing white blouse that hung off her shoulders in a sharp cut, and dropped down into a deep V, the scant view of her breasts just barely hidden.

"Sei un'opera d'arte," I whispered by the nape of her neck, my lips skimming her skin as I slowly trailed my finger lightly down the front of her chest. She shuddered at the chill it gave her, and I laughed when goosebumps rose on her arms.

In one quick movement, my hands pulled at her tights by her inner thighs, the sound of clothes tearing filling the space. She let out a cute gasp at my audacity, but before she could protest, I stole a kiss.

"Hope you weren't too attached to that pair of tights," I quickly told her.

She didn't even have time to answer before my thumb was already tracing circles on her clit.

"Naughty girl, *dolcezza*. Were you not wearing panties all day?"

Her voice came out raspy and breathless when she finally whispered, "I almost never do."

I bit my bottom lip at the image of Emilia day in and day out in her outfits, her bare pussy exposed, and I smiled at how filthy my woman was.

I circled harder, letting two fingers slide into her wet heat. She was drenched already, and I used her own lubrication to tease her, driving her wild. My strokes were slow and deliberate, and I could feel her getting impatient. She gripped my shoulders and started to take more pleasure for herself, driving her hips down onto my fingers, trying to find that release I knew she was craving.

"Do you want to come?"

"Mhm," she mumbled, her lips barely opening.

I glided her slickness to her clit, my fingers making a circular motion, and when I slipped my fingers back inside her, I sneaked one towards her ass, the tip of my finger nudging her entrance, begging to be let inside. When her cunt tightened its hold around my fingers and I felt her body start to relax, I stretched her open with my finger.

"I promise one day, Emilia, I'm going to take that tight ass of yours."

She whimpered in response, her cunt squeezing the life out of my fingers.

"You like the sound of that, dirty girl?"

"Fuck, Matteo, I'm going to come," her moan sounded so hot in my ear.

I pulled out of her before she can find her release and lifted her by her ass and flipped us, so she was spread out underneath me.

"The first place you're coming tonight is on my tongue. I need to taste you."

And then I hiked up her skirt and glided my tongue from bottom to top, giving her a nice little love bite on her clit, before I thrust my tongue inside her. Her cries of pleasure drove me forward as her symphony of moans graced my ears with the most beautiful song.

"Matteo!" she screamed, and on the tail end of my name, she detonated on my tongue. I licked up every drop of her, not wanting anything to go to waste.

I'd missed her. I'd missed her bratty mouth, and I'd missed that sweet taste of her.

"Tonight, I'm going to take my time with you. Take my

time loving you, loving your body. You're going to know what it feels like to be worshipped."

And I did just that. I memorized every inch of her skin. I spent hours just kissing and licking parts of her body until she was squirming beneath me. Touch wasn't enough for her, but I savored it. I tracked every blemish on her skin, every kiss on her body that drove her insane. I studied her intricate tattoos, imprinting them into my memory, imprinting her. Something about tonight felt different, and I think she knew that too. We spent the night kissing and touching, and we made love for hours, but we also held each other and talked about the better parts of our childhoods, reminiscing on our homes in Italy and what we missed. We spent our night as if tomorrow didn't exist.

And when she fell asleep, satiated and content in my arms, I treasured the moment for the days to come.

CHAPTER THIRTY-TWO

EMILIA

Last night felt bittersweet. Matteo still slept soundly under me, my head still resting on his chest. He had one arm wrapped possessively around my waist and his other hand had found its way into my hair. I tilted my head up gently so as not to disturb him.

He'd spent the better half of last night following through on his word. Every single part of my body was deliciously sore, and even now, hours later, my pussy still throbbed from where he had been.

His eyelids fluttered rapidly, and I took the opportunity to cherish this moment. I told Benji I was prepared to do whatever it takes, but laying in bed now with Matteo I almost wanted to go back on my word. I envied a life where I could wake up naked, twisted up in the sheets with him, not worrying about whether or not someone was going to try to kill me today or having an enemy breathing down my neck.

In another life, Matteo and I would go out into the city, go on dates and be another one of those couples to our peers. The kind of couples that can't stop finding each other across the room, hopelessly in love, silently speaking to each other in a language no one else knew. Spending our nights holed up inside, exploring each other's bodies. I envied that version of Emilia and Matteo.

But today, today was the day I was going to bring the fight to Camila.

I snuggled deeper into Matteo's chest, committing his smell and the feeling of the strong stature of his body as he protected me, even in his sleep, to memory. I didn't dwell long in my fantasy, because I knew if I did, I'd change my mind. And I didn't want to.

Matteo chose that moment to wake up. He gradually opened his eyes, and when they found mine, he looked briefly stunned, but it lasted a millisecond before his eyes filled with relief and his body relaxed.

"Il mio tesoro."

I couldn't help the smile that crossed my face at the endearment.

"Good morning."

He stretched out underneath me, before pulling me closer into his chest as he turned toward me so we were face to face.

"I'm surprised you stayed the night."

"That makes two of us," I admitted out loud to him.

He didn't seem shocked by my honesty at that, just took it in stride. He pulled me on top of him so I was straddling his hips, and then he lifted up to a sitting position. His arm snaked around behind my back and pulled me in closer to him as his other hand traced small teasing circles on my upper thigh. I could feel his hardening length underneath me, the tip of it brushing against the bare skin of my ass.

His lips grazed mine, his tongue lightly skimming them, pleading for entry. I parted my lips slightly, and he took advantage of the movement and his tongue dived in, sweeping the inside of my mouth, dueling with my tongue. I moaned into the kiss, grinding my hips downward into his lap, and I felt the pulse of his cock. He wasted no time maneuvering his body and slid his cock into my soaked cunt.

"Emilia," he begged in a strained whisper.

I pressed my body closer to his, laying my hands on top of his shoulders to gain better balance as I rode his cock relentlessly, chasing that high, that release. He thrust upward into me, meeting me stroke for stroke, driving in deeper until he was filling me completely. We were both panting as we pushed ourselves to our climaxes. The sensation of his cock overwhelmed my senses.

"Matteo," I whimpered, my eyelids fluttering closed. I threw my head back and I shattered around him, crying out his name one more time.

It wasn't long before he was filling me with his release, *il mio tesoro* falling from his lips.

We stayed there for a bit, him seated inside me as we attempted to catch our breaths. I knew he knew something was different, that something seemed off with me, but I couldn't dwell on it for long.

I lifted myself off of him and reached over the bed to start gathering up my clothes, and when I looked back at Matteo, he was sporting a shit-eating grin on his face.

"What's that look for?"

His smile grew wider on his face as he answered, "I love having you full of my come, that's all."

My eyes rolled as I laughed at him, shaking my head.

I dragged him over to the shower and we stood there under the hot steady stream of water, just wrapped up in each other's embrace. He was quiet for a bit, just enjoying the peaceful moment and the constant hum of the shower running.

"I won't let anything happen to you today, Emilia," he boldly promised me. I knew it was futile, just as Dante's promise was. I knew my men would take a bullet for me, would give up their lives for mine. That was what every mafia leader wanted—unwavering loyalty. But I loved all of them like family, and I couldn't bear to lose more of my family.

I didn't try to argue with him as I lied to his face, "I know."

*All day, my men and I had been preparing for a firefight. Just as I had predicted, news channels have picked up on the story of *La Corredora*'s men being slain by the docks. My message was heard loud and clear across the entire country, so wherever Camila was hiding out, I knew she'd make an appearance soon. If there was one thing I knew about Camila, is that she didn't like the attention on her. It messed with her business.

I had no idea where she and her men would pop up, but we needed to plan for anything. We were all congregated inside the foyer, and I scanned all of them, taking them in one at a time.

They were all covered head-to-toe in protective gear. Ballistic helmets sat on their heads, layered with a built-in flashlight, night vision goggles, and comm mics. Their bullet-proof vests had numerous pockets filled to capacity with magazine rounds, flashbangs, stun grenades, and knives, with a steel plate nestled behind it protecting the shield from rifle rounds.

I watched as Dante took command of my men, going over last-minute details with them. Not one inch of skin was exposed. Thick cut-resistant gloves covered their hands, and pads guarded their knees and elbows.

Strapped to each of their backs was an assault rifle with red dot sights and night vision optics, while two handguns lay on their hips.

When I joined them in my foyer dressed similarly, all of their heads snapped in my direction, waiting for further instruction.

"*La Corredora* and her men have been spotted over at the abandoned Vanmore estates, just on the outskirts of the city,

---

* Fallout - UNSECRET, Neoni | Spotify Playlist

which is good for us. No civilian casualties. We don't need to
worry about anyone getting caught in the crossfire."

"The estate with its own airstrip in the back?" Matteo
piped up.

"The very same," I told him. "There's only one entrance
in from the main road, but Camila may flee if she feels like
she's outnumbered, which is why that airstrip needs to be
watched."

"Dante, you, Antony, Stefan, and Leo will breach the front
entrance, while Matteo, Nico, Lorenzo, and I will follow in
from the back. Tobias will be stationed out in the trees,
informing us if Camila decides to escape through the airstrip.
Everyone knows their assignments?"

When they nodded in response I continued.

"Good," I said, nodding. "No one makes it out alive."

We took two armored cars toward the old Vanmore estate,
the drive only taking twenty-two minutes. I counted every
minute on the drive there, my thoughts on overdrive and the
hairs on my skin on edge. From the outside, no one could see
the anxiety coursing through my veins, but on the inside, every
fiber was going haywire.

We parked about a mile down the road, and hid the vehicles behind tree cover. After exiting the vehicles, I took a look
around at my men and I silently sent a prayer that they all
returned safely after this was over with.

"Godspeed," I told them, and with one last look or small touch of courage, we split into two groups.

We traveled the rest of the way on foot, covering the woods faster than I expected. Within ten minutes we were crouched low behind trees, staring up at the old estate. The light from inside was minimal, but when I aimed my assault rifle and peered into the night vision eye scope, I scanned the outskirts and counted six men.

Without lowering my weapon, I informed my men of the number and their locations.

I talked into the comms and internally I counted down on the clock.

"Tobias. Take them out," I ordered.

It was not long before I saw Camila's men drop like flies one by one as Tobias fired off shot after shot. He had a silencer on his sniper rifle so no shots echoed in the night, but I knew it wouldn't be long before command checked in and they didn't respond. It was now or never.

"Report in, Dante."

"We're in position," his response came in clearly.

"Breach." And then I led my charge through the cover of night.

CHAPTER THIRTY-THREE

MATTEO

"Breach," Emilia ordered Dante, and then she was off running toward the estate. I wasted no time following her, hot on her heels as we skirted the perimeter of the empty inground pool. Shots were fired inside the mansion and Emilia picked up her pace. Lorenzo and Nico were branched out on either side of us as we stepped onto the back terrace space.

It irritated me that Emilia was putting herself on the front lines, when a part of me wanted her far away from the action. I couldn't get distracted, but I knew I would be. I kept her within my peripheral vision at all times, not wanting her out of my line of sight. I knew I couldn't keep her away from this fight, not unless I was to tie her up, which I knew wouldn't bode well for me.

Last night felt like a dream. Some inner part of me felt like it wasn't real. But, it was. *She* came looking for me. And though I knew I had my work cut out for me when it came to winning her trust back completely, it would be worth it all. She was worth it all. I just wished she had let either of me or Dante lead the charge. With her in the lead, she was the first one in the line of fire, and that grated on me.

The old Vanmore estate was a mixture of modern architect meets old school money. The entire back of the house was floor to ceiling glass windows, and from our vantage point, we could see into the whole back half of the mansion.

Which is how we saw five men come barreling from what looked like a dining room at one point.

Shots rang out and it was pure chaos.

To my left, Emilia and Lorenzo sought cover behind dilapidated Greek columns and popped out sporadically to return fire. I saw an assault rifle aim in my direction and I dropped quickly to the ground, crawling toward an upturned oak table. Crouching behind the table, I popped up briefly, returning fire at my attacker. I knew I'd hit my mark when the bullets stopped flying my way.

Peeking out from the sides, I saw Emilia and Lorenzo still locked in their fight, but Emilia's bullet ripped through one of Camila's men's skulls and, as if in slow motion, I watched as his body pitched forward and he fell on his face, dead before he even hit the ground. Lorenzo moved into position away from the pillar and fired his weapon. His bullet hit the last guy standing, but not before he returned fire and hit Lorenzo square in the chest. Lorenzo went down.

I could see from my hiding spot as Emilia's eyes widened in panic and she jumped out into view with no coverage and grabbed Lorenzo by the back of his vest and struggled to pull him back behind cover.

I covered her as more men poured into the room, bullets flying from my and Nico's guns.

She managed to drag him back out of view as I made my way over to them.

"Lorenzo," she shouted, shaking him.

Slowly he tore his eyes open, a dazed look on his face. He ripped the steel plate out from behind his vest, and buried in it was the round that would've killed him where he stood if it weren't for the plate. We collectively sighed in relief and with a brief nod, we turned back to the fight where Nico had been desperately trying to cover us, popping in and out from where he was shielded.

It felt like an hour had gone by as we forced our way through the mansion, but I knew it had to be only ten minutes.

It was then that Tobias's voice came through the comm system.

"Camila is escaping through a side exit with five of her men," he informed all of us, and out of the corner of my eye, I saw Emilia's head whip in the direction of the woods where the airstrip would be. She bolted in that direction and I soon followed.

I yelled back into the comms over the heavy sound of bullets flying, "Emilia and I are in pursuit of Camila."

Emilia's voice came through the communications next.

"Hold the line in here, Dante. Tobias, take out her men, but leave Camila to me."

*Emilia and I ran through the back, the sounds of our heavy footfalls crunching over the newly fallen leaves as we chased after Camila.

I saw two of Camila's men fall, but Camila and the other three of her men made it into the tree cover and Tobias confirmed over the line he had lost visual. It was now on me and Emilia to handle the others.

Emilia and I are shoulder to shoulder as we race through the woods, dodging tree limbs and jumping over upturned roots. We were turning the corner when one of the men jumped out at me in my blindspot and tackled me to the ground. Emilia's pace faltered as she hesitated, but I waved at her to go. She looked back over at me with regret in her eyes, but took back off after Camila. I didn't have time to weigh what that look was about, as a fist flew at my face. My helmet was lost in the scuffle, and my rifle lay just out of reach. The

* Empires - Ruelle | Spotify Playlist

226

man on top of me aimed his pistol at my head, and I reached up, grabbing his wrist and knocking it sideways just as a shot rang out inches from my ear. The sound was deafening.

I was instantly thrown back into the past, images of that day playing in the back of my mind, while I struggled with the man on top of me. I heard another shot ring out, but this time it's from the direction where Emilia ran off. With my other hand, I pulled my knife and slid it into the man's neck so quickly he didn't even realize it's there, until I was ripping it from his throat. He dropped his gun, both hands flying to his throat as if he could stop the blood from pouring out. I didn't wait for life to leave his eyes; he'll be dead in seconds.

Grabbing my assault rifle and helmet, I took off in Emilia's direction, calling out to her via the comms, when I noticed that in the tackle, my comms had been destroyed.

With fear in my heart, I pushed my body faster toward her. My eyes felt like they were looking through a fuzzy lens, and I could still hear the echo of the gunshot ringing in my ear. But no matter how disoriented I feel, my body refused to stop.

I heard more gunfire ring out in the night, closer than before, and then silence. I was in the clearing now, the view of the airstrip in front of me lit by minimal floodlights from the watchtower. Emilia stood over a body with a gun aimed at their head. I saw Emilia's lips move before I saw a flash and then the person didn't move.

Emilia stood there frozen, her helmet on the ground and her arm limply at her side. I started to make my way over to her when I heard it. A shot rand out in the distance and I recognized it for what it was—a sniper shot—and everything in me was paralyzed. It all happened in slow motion.

The bullet ripped through Emilia and she fell to her knees.

I was by her side instantly, dragging her behind the safety of the watch tower, calling into the comms that Emilia had been hit only to remember in utter horror that they were broken and her comms was laying just out of range.

I peered down at her, and my heart ceased to beat. There was blood everywhere and when I pulled off the vest, I saw the bullet lodged in her chest. She was struggling to breathe, her arms clawing at my chest, begging me to help her.

"Fuck!" I screamed into the dead of the night. "Stay with me, love," I pleaded with her. "You're okay, you're okay," I said over and over again.

She needed a hospital immediately. There was nothing I could do to help her.

"Emilia, I need you to keep fighting," I told her. "I'm going to get you out of here."

I frantically looked around, hating myself for letting my comms get destroyed, but hating myself more knowing that I needed to leave her in order to save her.

"I'll be right back," I said and I watched as her once vibrant blue eyes dimmed in color.

"Fuck!" I screamed once more as I raced out of the watchtower, sprinting toward her helmet, waiting for the shots to ring out, but I made it back to the watchtower and yet no shots.

I didn't have time to ponder why that was, all I cared about wasEmilia and keeping her alive. I heard Dante's voice come in on the line, sounding out of breath.

"Emilia! Matteo! Where is your location?" he shouted over the line.

"Watchtower!" My voice was clipped. "There was a sniper hidden in the woods. Emilia is down. Dante, it's bad. We need air support or she won't make it."

I reached Emilia and cradled her body in my arms, her skin clammy and cold to the touch. Her eyes were fading and I could tell she was on the edge of unconsciousness.

I heard Dante cursing over the line song with her other men. I could hear them running through the woods, Dante's voice calling in for air support and our location, but I feared they wouldn't arrive in time.

"And Camila?" Dante said over the comms system.

"Gone," I muttered in defeat.

If Emilia died, it was all for nothing. And I didn't think I'd ever forgive myself. More swearing came over the radio, but I tuned them out and focused on Emilia.

When her eyelids started to flutter close, I shook her.

"Emilia, baby, stay with me."

She started to shake and I knew she was going into shock. I put pressure on her wound as best as I could.

"You can't leave, Emilia. Not like this," I begged. "I'm not too proud to say that I need you. I love you, Emilia," I told her. "And I need you to fight like hell to stay alive because I need you to be here so that I can show you every day how much I love you."

I heard the faint chops of wind from the helicopter in the distance.

"Hear that, Emilia? Help is here. You're going to be okay."

She squeezed my hand tightly, and I leaned down as her lips opened to talk.

"Matteo," she choked out. "I…"

But I didn't get to hear what she had to say. Just as Dante barged in with paramedics, her eyes closed and her hand went limp in mine and I let out the most guttural cry.

CHAPTER THIRTY-FOUR

EMILIA

*I HEARD THE SHOT BEFORE I FELT IT. WHEN THE BULLET ripped through my chest, I instantly felt like I was underwater, drowning, but I was on fire at the same time. I didn't remember much after that except the blood and pain. There was so much of both.

Matteo was there, I think. His face was blurry and was in and out of focus. When he was in focus he had the most devastated look on his face and there were tears running down his cheeks.

He kept talking to me, but I couldn't hear him. All I could see were his lips moving frantically. The pain was etched into his face and it was the most disturbing thing to see.

I didn't like to see him in pain.

I felt tired, and now I was shaking as if I'd submerged myself into Lake Michigan in the dead of winter.

Why was I freezing?

I heard muffled shouting in the distance, but all I could focus on was Matteo.

I wanted to tell him that I was sorry for everything. That I

---

*   Deep End - Ruelle

wanted to fight so bad. I wanted to fight for him, for us. But, I was exhausted and I just wanted to sleep. I wanted to tell him everything.

I croaked out his name, the word feeling like gravel in my throat and it felt like my body was on fire. I struggled to breathe, but it felt like an elephant was sitting on my chest and suddenly I was choking. "I …" I managed to say, but I couldn't push the rest of the words out.

The edges of my eyesight started to blur. And then I saw nothing but black.

EPILOGUE
MATTEO

ONE YEAR LATER

BLOOD PAINTED MY HANDS, AND MY KNUCKLES WERE SPLIT wide open and bruised from the beating I'd unleashed on one of Camila's men. I've been angry for over a year now. I promised Emilia I'd protect her, and I failed.

*Time of death was 11:47 pm on November 17th.

I died that night right alongside her. When her eyes closed and she went limp in my arms, every single part of me shattered into a million pieces.

Dante still rushed her to the hospital in the helicopter, and I followed, numb and in shock. The paramedics felt a weak pulse, but she wasn't breathing. The doctors at the hospital only confirmed her death when we arrived.

DOA.

I hated those three letters side by side like that. When they said that out loud and her official time of death, I had lost it.

I had gone into a frenzy, and it took three of Emilia's men to subdue me and a heavy sedative from the hospital to put

---

* Hurts Like Hell - Tommee Profitt, Fleurie

me down. When I came to, I was no longer in the hospital, but back in the room I had at Emilia's estate.

The bed was still unmade from how we had left it from the prior morning, and when I awoke I was instantly assaulted by her scent.

I'd dropped to my knees and cried until there was nothing left in me, to the point that I had exhausted myself. I slept for the next forty hours.

The few days after her death, we all moved slowly, lost in a trance, trekking through mud. We were all in mourning and grieving in our own ways. There was tension in the air, and I think we all had blamed not only ourselves but each other for not being there to protect her.

Even a year later, the mystery sniper was still at large along with Camila, which was what led me to now, in this moment

I had made it my soul mission to continue Emilia's fight by going after Camila's gang. I wouldn't stop until she and every single one of her men were buried deep in the ground. Dante took over after Emilia's funeral, his focus primarily on keeping her businesses going and fending off reporters that showed up outside the gates. It had been her wish to have a closed casket.

He had changed the most, I think, besides me.

The day after her funeral, he told me about the conversation he'd had with her the night before she died about her wanting to find a woman named Gianna Hayek. Neither of us was sure why or what her reasoning was until Dante had discovered a letter written by Emilia.

In the letter, she stated that if we were reading this letter, it was because she was no longer here and that our mission had failed. She didn't want us to suffer, but she had no right to ask that of us.

I suffered every damn day she wasn't here. While Dante made it his primary focus to find Gianna and follow through with Emilia's last request for him, I couldn't find it in myself to do what Emilia had asked of me.

There was no world in which I would live that I would ever try to move on from her. No world that I could be happy in without her. I had just gotten her back, only for the world to be a cruel cunt and rip her away from me.

For an entire year I woke up, ate enough food to sustain me, hunted down Camila and her men, and slept. The next day, I'd just repeat the cycle.

I was a shell of a man with her gone. Even driving my car didn't fulfill me anymore. There were days I thought about ending it all and joining her in the afterlife, but I knew I couldn't leave this world without avenging her first.

I was cleaning the blood off my hands with a rag, when a call came through on my burner. The only two people who knew this number were Dante and Tobias.

Dante's name appeared on the screen.

He tried to check in with me weekly. Sometimes I picked up his calls, but most of the time I ignored them. But I had a feeling I should pick up this call.

"Dante," I addressed him with an edge in my voice.

"Matteo," he says, something off with his voice. It almost seems hopeful and cheery.

"What is it, Dante? I'm kind of in the middle of something."

I look down at the dead man now leaning over his restraints, and absolutely dreaded the next part of getting rid of the body. I had gained no intel I could use to my advantage to get anywhere closer to finding Camila.

"Have you seen the news?" his voice came in over the line.

He didn't wait for my response before the next words out of his mouth made me feel the first shred of emotion in over a year.

"Camila is dead."

"They're positive?" I questioned him. "You know how news outlets like to run with stories before knowing all the facts."

"FBI confirmed it this morning."

A huge sigh of relief filled my body at the news.

"Did they say how?"

"That's the strangest thing. They found her hiding away in one of her safe houses in Belize, a bullet in her head, execution style. I thought it was you," he says.

I wish it were me.

I heard footfalls in the hall behind me. I was in an abandoned factory out in the outskirts of Seattle, and no one knew where I was, not even Tobias.

I quietly pulled out my Glock, making my way to the door, when the footsteps halted. I threw open the dirty curtain that hung from the ceiling and scanned my surroundings. I didn't see anyone. I was definitely losing it. But then something caught my eye by my feet.

There, underneath my shoe, was an emerald ring.

My heart fluttered and then seized completely. I felt my heartbeat in my throat as I instantly recognized the ring. It was Emilia's. The one her father had given her, the one she never took off. I kept my gun raised, about to put a bullet in whoever was fucking with me because I knew she had been wearing that ring when she died. She had been buried with it. So who dug up her grave and was taunting me with it? Whoever it was, I was going to make them suffer.

Dante's voice was still talking in my ear, when I saw movement out of the corner of my eye. And if I thought my world was turned upside down a year ago when Emilia died, nothing could've prepared me for the sight in front of me.

"Dante," I said hoarsely when I could find the words. "I'm going to have to call you back."

And then I hung up on him, lowering my phone but not my weapon because I couldn't trust my eyes and what I saw before me.

Because standing a mere fifteen feet in front of me had to be a ghost or a hallucination, proof of my insanity.

But then the figure spoke.

"Hi, Matteo," Emilia said in a whisper.

EPILOGUE
EMILIA

ONE YEAR LATER

*"HI, MATTEO," I SAID IN A SOFT VOICE, SCARED THAT I'D spook him. He didn't lower his weapon, but rather, hung up on the person he was speaking with on the phone. Standing this close to him, I could see the damage my death did to him. For the past year, I'd been underground, only catching glimpses of him and the rest of my family through what the *Septem Daemonia* had shown me.

He'd lost muscle, and his eyes looked dead, devoid of life itself. His once animated, luscious forest green eyes have lost their spark altogether, and I knew I was to blame.

He stared at me in a daze, his eyebrows crinkled together as if he were trying to put together how I could be here in the flesh. Finally, when he spoke up, it was with disdain and confusion.

"I thought you were dead. I was there as they laid your casket in the ground. I grieved for you, still am," he scoffed.

---

* Close To You (Acoustic) - Brainheart, Anica

"And you appear out of thin air a year later and all you have to say is *Hi Matteo?*"

I put up my hands in surrender.

"I know it doesn't mean much and you're hurting, but it was the only way. I needed everyone I loved the most to believe I was dead in order for my plan to work."

"What plan?!"

I sighed, having dreaded this conversation for a year now.

"There's a lot I need to explain to you," I confessed.

"Then start talking," he demanded of me, not once lowering his weapon.

"The day that we met at the *This Side of Heaven* masquerade party, that was my initiation into a secret society called *Septem Daemonia.* Have you heard of it?"

He nodded his head in response.

"I've heard the rumors. You got the tap?" he asked incredulously.

"I did," I confirmed. "Envy was the sin I had selected. That was just the first test. I met with one of their own a few days later, but I hadn't made my final decision yet."

I took a deep breath, steeling myself for the truth. I briefly wondered if this was what Matteo had felt when he'd confessed to me about his contract with the FBI.

"It wasn't until I had you and Tobias and you told me you were sent undercover by the FBI into my ranks that I had decided to call them and make a deal."

"Those two days you were gone," Matteo replied, filling in the blanks.

"Correct."

"He asked me if I was prepared to do whatever it took, whatever the cost," I swallowed nervously. "I was. I couldn't have the FBI and Camila's gang breathing down my neck for the rest of my life, so I made a decision that I thought was right at the time."

"Right for who?!" he seethed.

"You have a right to be angry with me. Everyone does, but I needed to fake my death so the FBI would start to look at Camila and her cartel gang and take the eyes off of my men and businesses. And I also needed Camila to let her guard down and think I was dead. The second she did, I'd be there."

"How ... how did you do it?" he asked with an overwhelming sigh.

"The *Septem Daemonia*."

I swallowed as if there was gravel in my throat. Butterflies danced in my stomach, and not the good kind. I'd lived with the guilt of hurting the people I loved the most for a year, knowing that when I made that decision in the back of that car that night that I'd potentially lose their trust and never gain their forgiveness.

"I knew about the sniper in the woods," I admitted. "I positioned myself just right for him to take the shot. It was laced with a rare toxin to make it look as if my heart had stopped. From there it was a race to get me to the hospital, where their doctors would give me the antidote, and then the secret society took me and I went underground."

He didn't breathe. He didn't even move an inch. Matteo just stared at me, open-mouthed, his expression one of betrayal and awes.

"You knew?" Those two words leaving his mouth were like a knife to the heart.

I nodded, not able to find the words.

"You should've told me," he roared, the raw emotion seeping from every word. "Do you know what it was like watching you die?"

Tears ran down his face and mine were soon to follow as I brought my hand to my waist, like I could stuff my feelings down, but it was no use.

We stood before each other, both betrayed and hurt by the other's mistakes. We were both damaged and broken.

"There was blood everywhere and I was so goddamn helpless. I held you in my arms as you took your last breath, watched those baby blue eyes fade of your light and I died with you. You broke me, Emilia. I'm broken!"

"I am too, Matteo. I knew the second I made that decision I'd regret it because I knew that it meant lying to you and Dante and the rest of my family in the worst way. I knew the damage it'd cause, but I was ignorant of the fact that you'd all power through it and move on. Continue living your life without me ..."

He didn't let me continue.

"Move on from you?" he laughed, lowering his weapon for the first time and doubling over at the waist.

"There's no moving on from you, Emilia. I told you once that you were it for me, and I meant that."

"You're it for me too, Matteo. I want a life with you by my side."

"And what does that even look like for you, Emilia? You're dead to the world"

"The *Septem Daemonia* will slowly integrate me back into society with a whole backstory. I killed Camila and I knew you and Dante had looked out for our city and my girls. I'm coming home." I inhaled a deep breath. "I want to come home, Matteo. I want to come home to Chicago and I want you there."

"I don't know if I can," he stated.

I take a step back as if I had been shot. I had always dreamed about this moment. Finding Matteo and confessing everything to him, no more secrets between us and a chance to finally start a life together back in my home of Chicago. I'd never prepared for him to say no.

"That night I was scared to death. I took a big chance in the *Septem Daemonia* and their ability to revive me. I had no idea if those truly would be my last moments here on Earth, but I knew I couldn't leave until you knew how I felt about you. You had asked me once if I felt the same and blatantly called me out on my bullshit. You saw right through my lie that night. I knew at that time I was falling in love with you too, and that night as you held me only solidified that for me, and I knew it was too late."

I attempted to draw closer to him, one step at a time. He didn't retreat, so I took another step towards him.

"I love you, Matteo Ricci. And now I'm making a promise to you, as you did to me. I promise you that from this day forward there will be no secrets between us and I'll spend every day showing *you* how much I love you if you come back to Chicago with me, because while I can do this without you, I don't want to. I don't want to live without you."

I was standing barely a foot apart from him, close enough that I could reach out my hand and touch him, and God, did I desperately want to touch him. I'd missed the feel of his skin on mine, I'd missed the things his tongue did to me, and I'd missed the sensation of being wrapped up tight in his arms, protected.

He swallowed roughly, and I watched the motion of it as it moved down his Adam's apple.

"You love me?" he finally asked.

"I love you," I confirmed for him.

And then he was lunging for my face with both hands, his lips crashing into mine and it was explosive and euphoric. We were fumbling for each other, hands roaming every body part that we could touch, making up for lost time.

When we both came up for air, we were panting heavily.

"Don't ever leave again, Emilia. I'll follow you to the grave, you hear me?"

"I hear you, Matteo."

He cradled my head in his hands, our foreheads touching, our breaths in perfect sync as we cherished this moment together.

"You have a lot to catch me up on," I told him.

He laughed, and it was the best sound in the world, a sound I'd treasure forever.

"We've got plenty of time."

"So now what?" he asked.

I smiled up at the man before me. A man who'd infiltrated not just my family, but my heart. Matteo gave me hope. He was the light in the darkness and for the first time in my life, I was starting to know what happiness felt like.

"Now we love each other to our hearts' desire."

ACKNOWLEDGMENTS

Almost an entire year later and I find myself writing another acknowledgement page. It is amazing what can happen in a year's time. This past year has introduced me to so many new readers and fellow authors, and I have been blessed with so many opportunities I never thought I would get, so thank you —from the bottom of my heart.

Thank you to the most supportive family for showing up to every book signing event to name dropping me to everyone you know to read my books. I appreciate you guys more than you'll ever know.

To my bookstagram friends, a million thank you's for letting me bounce around ideas to you and helping me get this book to what it is today. I truly have the dream team.

To all those who will pick up this book, thank you. I hope you find yourself in my characters. I hope you realize that you are never too much for the right person. I hope that you always fight for yourselves, and to always look out for one another. In a cruel world, I hope you always choose to be a person's light in the darkness.

It's a very surreal feeling calling myself a published author, but it has been the highlight of my entire life, and I truly love what

I do. I hope to create more stories about unhinged villains and their happily ever afters for you in the years to come, so thank you once again reader for taking a chance on a new indie author.

ABOUT THE AUTHOR

Born and raised in a small town in Connecticut, Leslie Bates always had her nose buried in the pages of a book.

Leslie is an author who works full time helping couples make their most special day, a day to truly remember as a wedding coordinator.

She is a dark fantasy/romance writer who loves a good villain story with just the right amount of spice and morally gray characters. When she's not writing her newest story, you can catch her exploring the world one passport stamp at a time, curled up with a good book, or spending time with family and friends.

For updates on future projects, follow her on social media and on her website, www.lmbates.com!

instagram.com/_butfirstbooks

tiktok.com/_butfirstbooks

amazon.com/stores/author/B0DJMMN838

goodreads.com/lesliebatesauthor

www.ingramcontent.com/pod-product-compliance
Lightning Source LLC
Chambersburg PA
CBHW031214260626
47169CB00007B/2054